Published by Pleasant Company Publications
Text copyright © 2003 by Megan Shull
Illustrations copyright © 2003 by Pleasant Company
All rights reserved. No part of this book may be used or
reproduced in any manner whatsoever without written
permission except in the case of brief quotations embodied
in critical articles and reviews. For information, address:
Book Editor, Pleasant Company Publications,
8400 Fairway Place, P.O. Box 620998, Middleton, WI 53562

Special thanks: Noni Korf Vidal, Lindsay Eisenhut, Cornell
University, Jane Greenberg, Gary Hodges at Jon Reis Studio,
Ithaca Girls' Hockey, Keith Kubarek, Middleton Cycle and
Fitness, Digit Murphy, Ann Rollo, Katie Waller.
Ithaca kids: Alex T., Alex Y., Alexis, Anna, Brandon, Carlee,
Connor, Delevan, Eamon, Emily, Gabe, Hannah, Jamie,
Joseph, Jordan, Kevin, Kris, Laura, Lauren C., Lauren N.,
Lindsey, Maia, Maya, Plume, Rell, Safira, Sarah, Siera.

Printed in the United States of America
03 04 05 06 07 RRD 10 9 8 7 6 5 4 3 2 1

The characters and events in this book are all fictional. Any
similarity to a real person, living or dead, is coincidental
and not intended by the author.

Library of Congress Cataloging-in-Publication Data

Shull, Megan.
Yours truly, Skye O'Shea / by Megan Shull.
p. cm.
Summary: Eleven-year-old hockey sensation Skye O'Shea
deals with boys, sisters, math tests, team tryouts, and other
ups and downs of middle school.
ISBN 1-58485-768-4
[1. Schools—Fiction. 2. Hockey—Fiction. 3. Family life—
Fiction.] I. Title
PZ7. S55942 Yo 2003   [Fic]—dc21   2002007676

The best times of your life
have not yet been lived.

Yours Truly,
Skye ☺'Shea

BY MEGAN SHULL

For Alice
and the little angels,
with love

Many thanks to Pleasant Rowland for reminding me the sky is the limit; to the folks at Pleasant Company, especially Judy Woodburn, Will Capellaro, and my amazing editor, Therese Kauchak; and to my superstar team at ICM—my agent, Richard Abate, and attorney, James Gregorio. Special thanks to the Matyas family for the sweet Shangri-la on Cayuga Lake. And to all the gracious people in Ithaca and beyond who light the way—my parents, family, and friends—thank you from the bottom of my heart.

Wear a Helmet

I will never admit this to anyone else, but in September, when I entered the illustrious halls of Lakeview Middle School, I became afflicted with a major case of "boy on the brain" (Paige's term). It's a serious condition. Don't get me wrong—I don't hang out in my room and make out with my pillow or do "lip push-ups" against my hand. But I do spend quite a few of my waking hours thinking about Ashton Fergesen, the most exquisite specimen of boy in the entire sixth grade. He has this surfer-skateboarder thing going on, and his bleached-blond hair is just a little longer than most of the other boys' in my grade. Plus he's smart and mysteriously quiet. And if you're lucky enough to get up close to him, you will see his eyes are tie-dye blue—I swear.

The only class I have with Ashton is science, so in order for me to catch a glimpse of him any other time, I have to take matters into my own hands. When the bell rings after eighth period, I squeeze through the crowded hallway, and if I time it just right, I brush by Ashton next to the water fountain in front of Ms. Miller's room. I'm fine as long as I don't actually come into contact with him. When that happens, forget it. I get this spine-tingling jolt from my toes to my brain, and every ounce of blood in my body seems to make a mad sprint to my head. I might as well also own up to the fact that the tips of my ears turn hot, red, and tingly. But above all, I have to remember not to let my look linger. Because, according to Paige, girls should always look away first. She reads these things in magazines.

"You have to evoke some mystery into the equation," she says, sounding like the advice columnist in some teen magazine. But all it takes is one smile from Ashton and my heart starts to thump fast and loud, like it's broadcasting over the Lakeview sound system:

"Attention, students! Skye O'Shea, the cute sixth-grade girl with straight brown hair, freckles, and a ponytail, has a major, big-time crush. Let's listen in on her heart: *tha-thump, tha-thump, tha-thump . . .*"

Last week in homeroom we are talking like we do every morning, our desks pushed together in a circle. Ms. Hahn is explaining to us how she hopes we all will think of homeroom as a safe place to talk about anything that's on our minds. Ms. Hahn is really nice and young and fun. I totally lucked out getting her as my teacher for both homeroom and language arts.

"I hope," Ms. Hahn says, looking right at me and smiling, "I hope this can be a safe haven from the hustle and bustle of sixth grade."

Josh Finkelstein is sitting next to me. His hand shoots up, like he's going to burst if he doesn't get called on this instant. He leans toward Ms. Hahn and raises his hand high, supporting it with his other arm as if that will help him get called on sooner. By the time Ms. Hahn finishes talking, Josh is practically keeling over.

"Do you have something you want to share, Josh?" Ms. Hahn asks.

Josh Finkelstein has gone to school with me since kindergarten, and, not to be rude or anything, he's kind of weird. He's always carrying around dice, and at lunch he plays Dungeons and Dragons on the stage by the cafeteria. Plus he has a bad habit of not combing his hair, washing his clothes, or wearing deodorant. All of these things do not help with Josh's popularity.

"I, I, I, I, I," Josh strains to speak. I am feeling very sorry for him because he has a bad stutter, and it's quite clear to me that he can't really help it. It's awkward. Everyone is waiting, wanting to jump in and finish his sentence. Except we don't know what he wants to say. After what seems like forever, Josh blurts it out, all in one big breath. "I heard this eighth grader on the bus say that Ashton Fergesen split his head open skateboarding and he's in the hospital and he might die!"

Up until this very moment, I am practicing my autograph all over the front of my yellow language arts folder. But when Josh says "he might die," I stop doodling and look up at Ms. Hahn. I am hoping she will say, "Well, that's just a rumor, Josh. I just saw Ashton in the hallway." But she doesn't.

My breath is gone.

My stomach drops to the floor.

My heart starts racing.

"Actually, Josh, I'm glad you brought that up. It gives us an opportunity to talk about it," Ms. Hahn says. "How many of you know Ashton?" We all raise our hands. Everyone knows Ashton—he's really popular and athletic and nice. Ms. Hahn continues. "I'm sorry to say Ashton was in a very serious accident this weekend."

I begin to feel really sick.

Ms. Hahn smiles gently, walks over to her desk in the front of the room, and leans against it. "All I can say right now is that Ashton is in the hospital getting the best care possible." She seems nervous when she says this, as if she's not totally sure what's going to happen.

I'm getting hot and sweaty.

My heart is pounding.

My stomach feels worse.

I hate it when anyone gets sick or hurt. I mean, even if it wasn't Ashton, I'd still be freaked. It seems like Ms. Hahn reads my mind.

"It's hard to concentrate on school when something like this happens, isn't it?" she asks, looking directly at me. "It's upsetting when someone we know gets hurt." All of us sit in complete silence. Even Jason Kendall—the most annoying kid in my homeroom, who always has something obnoxious to say—is speechless. "If anybody wants to talk more about this, they can go see Dr. Delaney in the guidance office," says Ms. Hahn. "Otherwise we are just going to have to send good thoughts to Ashton and hope for the best."

The bell rings and Ms. Hahn's tranquil voice is soon drowned out by students swarming the hallways, shuffling from homeroom to first period.

Funny Feelings

So the entire week, all I can think about is Ashton. And I don't worry like a normal person. I've never told anyone this, but when I worry, I get this really funny feeling that whatever I do will affect the person I'm worried about—as if his life or death lies entirely in my hands.

For example, when Ms. Hahn tells us about Ashton, I get this feeling that if I just don't walk on any of the cracks on the tile floors lining the Lakeview hallways, he will be OK. So for four days straight, I gingerly walk around every crack. And just for insurance, I close and open my locker door exactly seven times every morning. I don't know why seven—I just consider it to be a very lucky number, so seven it is. I'm sure this all sounds very strange.

After four days of driving myself completely crazy with my little rituals, everyone, including me, lets out a gasp when Ashton walks into science on Wednesday. A heavy plaster cast covers his hand, elbow, and shoulder. A long pink gash, complete with a neat row of ten black stitches, makes a line over his eyebrow. During the sixth-grade assembly I get a closer look. Our class is late because Mr. Hanson is so strict and neurotic, he makes us walk like we are in kindergarten: single file, no talking.

When we enter the front of the auditorium, the entire sixth grade is already seated, and everyone is waiting for our class to sit down. Dr. Hernandez is on the stage, looking down at us.

"Please," she says, "let's get the show on the road, people."

I scramble to find an empty seat, plop down in the middle of the front row, and tuck my folders under my chair. I glance to my left at Josh Finkelstein, dice and all, sitting beside me. Then I turn to my right and—

Ashton.

He is there.

Right next to me.

I stare straight ahead, like a horse with blinders on, while my stomach kicks into full churning mode. See, there's one minor thing I've sort of been leaving out about Ashton, and that's the fact that I've never actually said a word to him in my entire life. When he turns and smiles right at me, my stomach starts doing backflips and my heart begins to race. It is at this point that I begin to have a serious conversation with myself: *Self, do not freak out! Do not freak out!* But it's no use. My body chooses to ignore my head and the tips of my ears turn hot and tingly.

I try to pull myself together, concentrating all my will on Dr. Hernandez standing on the stage in front of us. But when the auditorium lights go dim and the slide show begins, Ashton leans over and says something. Yes, you read that right. He says something.

To me.

Only he is saying it so softly, I can't make it out. Plus, I'm not the type who likes to get in trouble, and even though it's kind of dark, I can clearly see Mr. Hanson in front by the stage, giving us a stop-talking-or-I-will-have-you-removed kind of look. This is not deterring Ashton. He speaks again, this time louder.

"Pretty boring, huh?" he asks. And then, before I even manage a smile, he reaches below my seat and picks up my green science note-book. He puts it on his lap, pulls out a pen from his pocket, and starts writing on the cardboard front cover. "Hey, Skye!" he writes with big puffy letters. "What's up?" Then around the word "Science" he doodles:

The lights flicker back on and I stare straight ahead at the speaker onstage. I pretend to concentrate, even though I *so* can't. Paige's voice is echoing through my head: *Don't look at him. Don't let him know what you're thinking, Skye!* What I'm thinking over and over again is how I need to act cool.

Act cool.

Act cool.

Please act cool.

But I do not feel cool at all. Sweat is accumulating under my armpits. And then, just as everyone starts clapping, signaling the end of the presentation, Ashton smiles mischievously and disappears into the rest of the sixth grade, funneling through the jammed doorway to race to seventh period.

A Real Kiss

I do not mention "the notebook incident" (as I will now officially call it) to anyone.

We are at lunch, sitting at a big round table in the cafeteria. I am sitting with my usual group: Paige, Emily, Lindsay, Winnie, Laura, Grace, and Olivia. I am staring at a toasted bagel with fluorescent orange melted cheese, wishing I had brought my lunch. We are all squeezed tight together, elbow to elbow, in major violation of Dr. Hernandez's new "four to a table" rule. We are talking about (surprise, surprise) boys. Of course, Paige is leading this discussion because she oozes cool. She's pretty and popular, and she's the only one of us besides Olivia who has any experience in these matters.

It is important to note at this getting-to-know-me stage that during these somewhat juicy conversations, I keep my mouth shut. The truth is—and I haven't really shared this with anyone—but I've never even kissed a guy. That's unless you count Danny Grady in third grade, who tackled me into the bushes by the jungle gym and slobbered all over me, smacking me on the lips. This is not exactly what I have in mind for a first kiss. Besides, according to Paige, it doesn't count as a real kiss unless both parties are "willfully participating."

One Week Later

My family is sitting around the square kitchen table eating dinner, like we do every night. And almost every night some type of drama erupts that is usually my fault. I interrupt someone, I talk with my mouth full, I use my fingers when I'm supposed to use my fork—pick your pleasure. Tonight is no different. As soon as Shannon kicks me in the shin under the table, I know there will be trouble. And even though her clunky shoe hits me right below the kneecap, I resist the urge to scream. Instead I shoot a quick look at my dad, who is busy carefully removing the bones from his salmon fillet, to make sure the coast is clear—and with one fluid motion, I kick my sister right back as hard as I can.

"You annoying little brat!" Shannon shouts, dropping her fork on her fish and lunging over the bowl of pasta salad to strangle me. I jump out of my seat and escape to the middle of the kitchen before she can inflict any more bodily harm. "Did you just see that?" she asks, shrieking.

This is as good a point as any to inform you that being the youngest of three girls is not, I repeat *not*, fun. My sister Shannon is the biggest faker in the entire universe. She stands up, clutching her shin in typical drama-queen fashion.

11

"That little brat just kicked me!" she says, very convincingly. I turn to look for some support from someone, from anyone. But everyone just stops eating and stares at me.

My dad is silent.

He is glaring at me.

He is fuming.

My mom lets out a big disappointed sigh, looks across the table at me, and shakes her head back and forth. My other sister, Shelby, immediately jumps to Shannon's defense. That's the problem with having older identical-twin sisters. It's two against one pretty much every day of my life. And everything, I mean every-thing, is *always* my fault.

"Skye, you are such a little brat," Shelby chimes in.

Great, a tag-team attack. They've both been a little mad at me since I *accidentally* deleted Shannon's American history paper on the computer.

Shannon sits back in her seat, continuing her award-winning performance, rubbing her leg and wincing in pain. Before I get punished for the rest of my life, I attempt to defend myself.

"She kicked me first—" I say. But it's no use. My dad turns to me. He's furious.

"Skye, since you can't act in a civilized manner, you may spend the rest of dinner in your room," he says, smoke billowing out of his ears. OK, there's no smoke, but he is looking ultra mad. Of course, as usual, he doesn't say a single thing to my sisters. They get off scot-free like always. I start up the stairs.

"She kicked me first!" I scream at the top of my lungs, tears cascading down my cheeks.

When I reach the top of the stairs, I look back down at my family. My parents are eating, and Shelby is, too. But not Shannon. She's looking up at me with an evil grin, her hand hidden under the table, waving me good-bye.

The Truth

When I get to my room, I slam my door as hard as I can. (This, by the way, doesn't make me feel any better.) I jump onto my bed, slip under my blue comforter, smush my face flat against my mattress, and bawl my eyes out. Everyone always thinks I'm lucky having twin sisters. They think Shannon and Shelby are so cool and that I always have someone to hang out with. Yeah, right. The truth is they really don't even talk to me, or let me wear their clothes, or tell me about boys, or, well, do anything big sisters are supposed to do. And to be totally honest, sometimes I think I'd be better off as an only child.

The only time my sisters and I even get along is when we play hockey. We all play. Hockey is what we're known for, I guess. If you ask anybody in town who knows our family, "What are the O'Shea girls like?" hockey is the first thing they will tell you about us.

And I will never, ever say this to Shannon and Shelby because of their already swollen heads, but my sisters happen to be awesome hockey players. They are good—*really* good. And someday soon I hope I'm that good, too. I'm not really big, super strong, or the best at every sport I play. But when I'm out on the ice, I feel special. And it's practically the only time

I can think of when I don't really think or worry about anything. I'm just in the zone, gliding.

The O'Shea family is a hockey family. Everybody knows my sisters, and soon everybody will know me. That is why, in exactly four days, I will be trying out for the Ithaca Comets fifteen-and-under girls' traveling hockey team. (Everyone calls it 15U.) Besides Ashton, making the Comets is just about all I can think of lately. I can't even tell you how badly I want to make this team. Since I'm only eleven years old, making the Comets is pretty much a long shot. My mom likes to point this out to me all the time.

"Just keep in mind that even if you do make this team, you might not get to play," she says. "I just want to make sure you realize this so you're not disappointed."

"I know, I know," I say back. "'Be realistic.' You've told me a thousand times." Obviously nobody else understands that I *have* to make it.

It's my destiny.

Three Days Later

You would think that because I come from a big-time hockey family, my parents would want me to ace Comets tryouts. But my family is totally weird. My mom and dad are obsessed with school, and it's completely annoying. "School always comes first"—this is my mom's favorite line.

Today before dinner, my mom starts lecturing me about this very topic. I am setting the table and she is standing at the kitchen counter by the sink, chopping onions. "Skye," she says, "your father and I are concerned that hockey is going to distract you from your schoolwork."

"You are so unfair!" I say, not-so-gently placing the silverware on the table. "I mean, you never say that to Shannon or Shelby." As soon as I say this, I kind of want to take it back. I know my mom hates it when I bring up my sisters like that. And this time's no different. She raises her voice over the onions now sizzling in olive oil on the stove.

"Shannon and Shelby aren't getting Ds in math, Skye," she says loudly. She manages to draw out "Ds" like "*Deeeeeeeeeees!*" to make her point. She is mad.

"Well, they are *so* your stupid little favorites!"

I say. OK, you're right. I don't say it—I'm not that crazy. I mean, I don't want to spend my entire sixth-grade life banished to my room. But I think it.

I finish setting the table and sit down at my seat. Don't get me wrong, it's not like I don't try in class or anything. School is just hard for me. It doesn't come easily like it does for my sisters. My mom adds chopped mushrooms and red bell peppers into the mix sautéing on the stove and turns down the heat. She walks over to the table and sits down beside me.

"Skye, it's not that we don't think you are fully capable," she says. "We are just concerned, and you need to be aware that your commitment has to be to school first, hockey second."

I make a face and look down at the floor.

"And don't roll your eyes at me, Skye. I don't appreciate that," she says, getting up and returning her attention to the stove.

Amazingly, I get through dinner without getting sent to my room. My dad only scowls at me once for speaking with my mouth full. Other than that, I survive without a scratch.

Five Hours Later

It's the night before Comets tryouts and I can't sleep. I've tried everything. Finally, at 1:11 in the morning, I go into my parents' room, where my mom proceeds to tell me it's just anxiety.

"Skye, it's normal to be anxious about tryouts, but it's not going to do you any good to worry," she whispers. "Just close your eyes and go to sleep!" She kisses me on the forehead, rolls over, and falls right back to sleep.

I trudge down the dark hallway back to my room. My superstitions appear to be in full bloom: It takes me an extra ten minutes to reach my bed, because if I don't leap over my hockey bag and land on my right foot—exactly one step away from my night table—I have to go back to the door and start over. Finally I do it just right on the seventh try, and I begin to worry that I might be a little crazy.

I turn on the small light beside my bed and try to read myself to sleep with the help of my science book's spine-tingling account of photosynthesis. But just as my eyelids get heavy, I have an overwhelming feeling that I might forget my skates in the morning. Since this happens to be a recurring nightmare of mine, I jump out of bed and double-check my gigantic red hockey bag for my size-six Bauer 4000s.

They are there (of course), tucked under my lucky jersey just where I put them. Then pure panic sets in—what if I forget something else? I kneel down on the blue carpet next to my hockey bag and stick my arm in, feeling around to make sure everything's there.

Helmet
Pants
Elbow pads
Shin pads
Socks
Garter belt
Shoulder pads
Red lucky number 17 jersey

It's all there. I crumble into bed. "Please let me make it. Please let me make it. Please let me make it." I say it over and over again, until I can't remember anything else and finally drift off to sleep.

Breathe

I am ready and waiting by the back door at exactly 5:30 the next morning when the headlights of Apple's mother's Volvo beam into our driveway. Mrs. Jensen (or "Summer," as she likes me to call her) decides to ease our nerves with a quick stop at the bakery. "Food will do a body good," she announces, smiling. We all get lemonade Snapples and toasted sesame bagels with cream cheese. We devour our food in the car on the way to the rink. We're done by the time Summer pulls up to the drop-off circle at the entrance.

"Go get 'em, girls!" Summer says with a big flashy smile. Apple is so lucky. She has one of those cool moms—you know, the ones who always look like movie stars, even when they first get up. The ones who say just the right things and never embarrass you in front of your friends.

I walk through the crowded lobby, my enormous hockey bag slung over my shoulder. People I don't even know nod hello to me and smile.

"What do we have here?" a tall, bald man asks as I walk by. "It's the littlest O'Shea!" All the parents stare at me. I am certain everyone is wondering if I'm as good as my sisters.

We finally wade through the busy lobby and

swing open the door to the crowded locker room. A maze of multicolored hockey bags clutters the floor. There's not even enough room for Apple and me to walk in, let alone put on our skates. We turn around, head back to the lobby, and plop down on the wooden bench next to the soda machine. Apple buckles on her goalie leg pads and chest protector. I slip on my skates and tighten the laces—first my left skate and then my right. I pull my lucky number 17 jersey over my head and glance around the lobby at the other players getting dressed. Everyone looks so good, and big, and old—and here I'm only eleven. My heart begins to thump fast and loud, and butterflies flutter in my stomach. I bend over and carefully tape each ankle, and I begin to feel like I'm going to throw up. I sit back on the bench and take a look around the busy lobby, now filled with a dozen players who are fully dressed in hockey gear and anxious to get out on the ice.

You can do this! I tell myself as I slide my helmet over my stars-and-stripes bandanna. I snap the chin strap tight under my jaw, grab my stick, and get up to join the other players standing by the door to the ice.

Everyone is bunched at the door, waiting for the Zamboni to make the final lap. Finally the door opens and we file out like ducks in a row, one by one, stepping onto the ice. As the blades of my skates cut into the ice and the familiar cool air streams through my face mask, all my worries seem to magically vanish. With each stride I begin to feel stronger and more confident, as if I can do anything. We all skate around, stretching and trying to impress the four coaches huddled together at center ice. Each coach is wearing a Comets' blue and gold warm-up suit. I try not to look directly at them as I skate by. Three guys I've never seen before are helping Lauren Carter-Johnson, the assistant coach who's running tryouts. Lauren stands in front of the guys, reads off her clip-board, and points to different spots on the ice, probably explaining the torturous plans she has in store for us.

Gaining speed, I round the far corner of the ice and spot Coach Cosgrove, the head coach, high up in the stands. He is wearing the same blue and gold warm-up suit and is writing something down on a clipboard. When the whistle blows, everyone hustles to center ice and forms a half circle around the coaches.

"Good morning, girls!" Lauren says, facing

us. The other coaches are lined up beside her. Lauren Carter-Johnson was my sisters' coach when they were on 15U. Her long black hair is pulled back in a ponytail and covered with a perfectly broken-in blue Comets baseball cap. Heart-shaped earrings dangle from her ears, and a shiny silver whistle hangs around her neck. She is really cool, nice, and funny. And she's a good coach, too. Everybody listens when she begins speaking.

"Girls, I'm going to tell you a big secret right from the start," Lauren says, pausing to look around. "The number-one thing you can do to help your chances is—"

Everybody leans in, eager for Lauren's advice.

"—to relax," Lauren says. "Just try to relax and have fun out here this morning."

I look around and take a deep breath—in through my nose and out through my mouth, just like they teach you in gym.

"Coach Cosgrove and I are looking for girls who can relax under pressure. We want players who know how to work hard and have fun," Lauren says. She is smiling right at me. I nervously smile back. "I wish you could all make the team. Unfortunately, we have room on our roster for only fifteen players." With this news there are loud gasps and whispers. "That's right," Lauren says, acknowledging what everyone is thinking but apparently is too afraid to say. "There are fifteen spots and thirty-seven girls trying out."

The rink echoes with shuffling skates. The air feels tense and heavy, like everybody is holding her breath.

Lauren continues. "That means you are going to have to work really hard to make this team. *No spots are guaranteed.*" I shoot a look around at the other players. The two girls on either side of me are fidgeting on their skates. I am not the only one who's nervous.

Karma

In the huddle, I recognize a couple of the other players from school, soccer, and lacrosse. I get the feeling they all know who I am, mainly because I have "O'Shea" stitched in big white letters across the back of my jersey. And everyone in Ithaca knows who my sisters are.

Lauren tells us to line up against the boards, count off by fours, and split up into the corners of the rink for a simple skating drill. I take a big breath and look around, relieved. I am grouped with the best skaters. I know this because most of the other girls in line with me are wearing the trademark gold Comets helmets, the kind the pro shop sells specially to girls who make the team. I am waiting for my turn when one of the best players, Logan Goldsmith, skates up behind me.

"Hey, little O'Shea! Good luck!" she says, smiling.

"Thanks," I say. I am feeling super cool now that Logan Goldsmith just acknowledged my presence.

But I don't feel super cool much longer. When it's my turn, I take three strides and fall flat on my face. This is not just a little fall; it's a big-time, everybody-sees-it kind of fall.

The girl behind me picks up my stick.

"Don't worry about it. I'm sure nobody even noticed," she says, handing it back to me. But they have definitely noticed.

"Way to go, O'Shea!" shouts one player I don't even know.

"Nice move, 17!" says another, laughing.

Humbled, I lean on my stick and lift myself up off the ice. I quickly peek up to where Coach Cosgrove is sitting to see if he has witnessed my fiasco. When I see he's talking to someone, his back turned away from the ice, I thank the gods for my good luck and hustle to the end of the line.

With ten minutes left in practice, I'm convinced my only hope for making the team is if I can really show my stuff in the final scrimmage. Lauren blows the whistle and lines us up against the boards in front of the players' benches.

"Listen, girls," she says, "we're going to scrimmage for the remaining ten minutes—"

"Yes!" says Logan.

"Awesome!" echoes this girl next to me in a green jersey. Her long red hair is dangling out of a shiny new gold helmet. I nervously rock back and forth on my skates, waiting for the next directions.

"Dark jerseys are with me," Lauren says, motioning for us to follow her into the far players' box. I look beside me, relieved to be standing next to Logan and Cash Erickson, another one of the best players from last year's team. I follow behind their matching gold helmets and sit down next to Logan on the long wooden bench. My head is racing a mile a minute. If I get to play with Logan and Cash, I'm set. I know I'll play great. I practically break into a smile as I glance up at Coach Cosgrove in the stands. But then Lauren glides over to our bench.

"Skye O'Shea," Lauren shouts, "you're centering Felicity and Marybeth."

What? Felicity? Marybeth?

So much for my perfect little plan. I roll my eyes and take a deep breath, exhaling loudly. I know this is majorly rude, but I already had to do a passing drill with Felicity and she can hardly skate. And one look at Marybeth's wobbling ankles and you'd feel sorry for me, too. How am I going to impress anyone with them on my line? I grudgingly get up, move down the bench, and plop down between Felicity and Marybeth. I am not happy, and it shows on my face.

"Hey," I say, turning to Felicity and faking a smile. But as soon as I lock eyes with her, my heart sinks. I have that feeling you get when you know you've been really mean and you want to take it all back, but you can't. And I'm pretty sure they both saw my snooty reaction to being on their line. So it serves me right when, on my first shift out, it's Felicity who gives me an absolutely perfect pass that leads to my only shot on goal in the entire scrimmage. I do not score. And I'm positive it's the universe paying me back for being so mean, snobby, and rude.

At the end of practice we huddle in a group at center ice. Everyone is resting on one knee, looking up at Lauren. "Good practice, girls," she says, smiling widely. "This is going to be a tough decision." Then she gets to the point we are all waiting for. "The names of the fifteen girls who make the team will be posted outside the front entrance to the rink in exactly six days. Any questions?"

Skates shuffle. You could hear a pin drop.

Logan finally breaks the silence. "You mean we have to wait the *entire week* before we find out if we made it?" she asks.

"That's torture!" Cash says.

Lauren just nods and smiles down at us. "Friday will be here before you know it. It will whiz by," she says. I start to skate away. "Oh, and one more thing—"

We all stop where we are and turn to look at

Lauren. "I hope all of you, regardless of what team you play on, have a fantastic season," she says. "Good luck, and great job today!"

By the time Summer drops me off at my house, I am sweaty and exhausted. It is only 8:00 in the morning. I'm home alone because my dad took my sisters to the Charles River tournament in Massachusetts and my mom is already at work at the hospital. I throw myself on the couch in the family room and flip through the channels on TV. Nothing good is on. I trudge upstairs with my bag full of stinky hockey gear, throw it on my floor, and climb back into my warm, comfy bed. I stare up at the ceiling and replay everything in my head a zillion times, trying to figure out if I have a chance of making the team. There are only two goalies trying out, Apple and Rachel McKenna. But there are a lot of forwards, and I'm the youngest. I attempt to make a special agreement with God.

"If I make it—" I say, my eyes closed tightly, "—if I make it, I'll never ask for another big thing again. And I'll be nice to everyone, even if they are really bad at something. I swear."

The Wait

I'm going completely crazy. My dad says he ran into Coach Cosgrove downtown. "Well, did he say anything, like if I made it or not?" I ask, eager for details.

"Sorry, pal, but all he said was 'hi.'"

"But was it a Skye-made-the-team kind of 'hi' or just a regular 'hi'?" I ask, scrounging for clues.

My dad peers out from behind the newspaper he is reading. "Skye, don't worry about things you can't control," he says before returning his attention to the paper.

Friday is an entire four more days away. I can't believe I have to wait this long.

Isabel

Lauren was wrong. This week is not whizzing by. I am attempting to get ready for school, but my sisters are hogging both upstairs bathrooms. I sit with my back leaning up against the door of my parents' bathroom and plead for Shelby to let me in.

"Open the door!" I shout. Nothing.

"*Pleaseopenthedooooor—*" I try again. "Come on, Shel! I have to brush my teeth!" I get up and kick the bottom of the door.

"Use the other one," Shelby finally answers. "This bathroom is occupied, Skye!"

Ugh! I head downstairs and wash my face in the tiny guest bathroom by the kitchen. It's a ghost town downstairs. Nobody's moving around but me. My mom left long ago for work and my dad teaches an early class this semester at the university. As usual, I find a note on the kitchen counter.

Skye,

Good morning! I had to leave early for work at the hospital.

English muffins + jam are in the fridge. Or you may <u>share</u> the last package of Pop-Tarts with your sisters! If you want to make your lunch, there's leftover mac + cheese. Help yourself. <u>Please</u> leave enough for your sisters. Have a great day, sweetheart!

Love, Mom xxoo

I crumple up the note and pitch a perfect three-point shot into the garbage. I walk over to the cupboard by the silverware drawer (where Mom hides all the really good snacks) and tear open the last silver-foiled package of strawberry Pop-Tarts. *What my sisters don't know won't hurt them,* I think. Plus, they always hog everything. I leave the Pop-Tarts in the toaster oven until the frosting on top is just a little brown, then toss them both on a plate. I eat fast and make triple-sure nobody is looking before I open the fridge and wash everything down with a big gulp of orange juice straight from the container. My dad would freak if he saw me do that. I run upstairs and throw my five main folders—along with my science, social studies, and math books—into my new blue backpack. The seams are already bursting. I struggle to zip it shut and head out the door for the bus.

I can see Isabel from our driveway. She's standing by herself, waiting for me in the middle of our empty street. I break into a slow jog to catch up with her. Isabel is by far the coolest neighbor in the world. In every way she is opposite my sisters.

Exhibit number one: She is nice to me.

Exhibit number two: She lets me wear her clothes anytime I want.

And exhibit number three: she even braids my hair sometimes before school.

And at Lakeview, even though she's in eighth grade and I'm only a measly sixth grader, she doesn't pretend she doesn't know me or act stuck-up, like lots of other eighth graders do. When I pass her in the hall, she waves, or shouts, "What's up, girl?" and flashes her trademark smile. Isabel is flat-out gorgeous. She's half Japanese (her mom) and half Brazilian (her dad). She has shiny reddish-black hair and smooth dark skin—she looks like she should be in an MTV music video, not in eighth grade at Lakeview. Isabel is by far the most popular girl in our entire school. And it's not just because she's beautiful. I think it's more because she's nice, funny, *and* smart.

I catch up to Isabel and we wait at the end of Kyle Kimber's brick driveway for the bus, along with everyone else from the neighborhood. When the bus finally pulls up, everyone lines up and files on. I sit down next to Paige, who is saving a seat for me, third row from the front. Isabel sits directly across the aisle from us with her best friend, Mackenzie Chase.

When the bus stops at a red light by the high school, the girls in the seat behind us start laughing hysterically. Everybody turns to look, and Paige and I do, too. When we peer over the top of the tall green bus seat, our gaze is met by a not-so-friendly-looking seventh-grade girl with straight, long blond hair and a pink polo shirt. The laughing comes to an abrupt stop. The girl leans forward toward us. She looks mad.

"Got a problem?" she asks, all huffy and rude.

"Sorry," I say, even though I have no idea what I am apologizing for.

Paige jumps in. "Listen, I don't know what your problem is."

My face starts heating up. I do not like conflict.

The blond girl's eyebrows scrunch up. Her cheeks are flushed red when she speaks. "Look, you stupid little sixth graders. You annoy me," she says. She is loud.

The entire bus is quiet. Everybody is staring.

"Why don't you two little brats turn around and mind your own business?" she asks.

Paige and I sink back down into our seat, mortified. And in case you've never had the opportunity to be humiliated in front of your entire bus, let me be the first to tell you—it's not fun. My face is completely red, and my stomach is queasy. Paige scoots over close to me. "What the heck is her problem?" she asks, rolling her brown eyes to make her point.

Then—to make matters worse—the bus driver, Mr. Deevers, looks back at us through the long narrow mirror above the steering wheel. He gets on the microphone. "Girls, is there a problem back there?"

You could hear a pin drop. Nobody says a thing.

Mr. Deevers keeps driving. I just sit. My stomach is tied up in knots. I happen to really hate it when people yell at me for absolutely no particular reason.

As we pull into Lakeview, Isabel leans over the aisle from her seat and whispers in my ear, her hand cupped over her mouth so nobody else can hear. "Just ignore her, Skye. Alexis Alexander is obviously completely jealous. You're one thousand times cooler than she is, and you're only in sixth grade," she says, emphasizing the sixth grade.

I am relieved that not everybody thinks we are annoying little sixth graders. Isabel always knows just what to say. And I am hoping, really hoping, that my day begins to get better soon.

Yellow Notes

My day does not get better. As I get up from
my desk to leave math class, Mrs. Mitchell walks
up and drops a yellow note on my desk. I've been
at Lakeview only a month, but it's pretty common
knowledge that yellow notes are not the kind of
notes you want to get from your teacher. I read
the note in the hallway outside Mrs. Mitchell's
room and stuff it in my pocket.

From the desk of Jane Mitchell
Lakeview Middle School

Skye,

Please see me before the end
of school today. We need to
discuss your recent homework
as well as what you are
planning to do about your
poor showing on your last
three quizzes! I will be
in my room at lunch.

Mrs. Mitchell

"The only negative things in my room are numbers!"

When there are fifteen minutes left at lunch, I
slip away from our table and walk down the empty
hallways into Mrs. Mitchell's room. She is alone,
sitting at her desk at the front of the room, grading

a big stack of papers. I am not trying to be rude, but she looks like the Wicked Witch of the West in *The Wizard of Oz*.

"Please come in," she says, not even looking up at me.

I walk in the room and stand beside her desk. She is still grading papers, and it's a good minute before she even stops what she's doing. She leans back in her chair and stares at me.

"I think we both know why you're here, Skye," she says, all creepy and mean. Avoiding her sorceress eye contact, I look out the window toward the lake.

"Ahhhh, well, I guess I'll have to come and get help?" I answer, stammering for words.

"That would be a start, Skye," says the sorceress. "Otherwise I'm going to have to give your parents a call."

Ugh. This is not fun.

The sorceress is still talking. "I know you can do this work, Skye." I glance at the clock, hoping time will pass faster, but it doesn't. She's still talking. "You need to make math a priority." Blah, blah, blah. "I doubt you would give up this easily in a hockey game, would you?"

When Mrs. Mitchell says "hockey," my ears perk up. I turn away from the window and look back at my teacher. "I need you to agree to work hard. And if you can't do your homework, come and get help. Is that agreed?" she asks.

"Yes," I answer, faking the tiniest of smiles, eager to get out of there as soon as humanly possible.

Mrs. Mitchell turns her attention back to the stack of papers on her desk. She does not say "good-bye" or "sounds good" or, well, anything. She just looks back down and keeps right on grading papers. And I know this is mean, but all I am thinking is that she is majorly weird, she can't teach math, and I can't stand her.

I leave the math room and sprint all the way back down the empty halls to the cafeteria, where I find my friends still sitting at our table, just the way I left them. Paige is retelling in detail the weird bus incident. I slip back into my chair next to Winnie and Lindsay. Olivia is saying that her older brother Brian says Alexis Alexander has serious problems—that she moved here from Michigan last year and she has a "major attitude." Winnie thinks we should sit next to her on the bus tomorrow, just to bug her. *No thanks*, I think to myself.

The bell rings and I just sit there at the table, my eyes closed and my head down, hoping this day will soon end.

The List

Friday is finally here. Sitting through eight hours of school is absolute torture. On top of that, I am convinced that if I just don't step on any cracks I will make the team—as if somehow, somewhere in the universe, stepping on cracks and my name being on the list are connected. And as crazy as this may sound, I do not step on one single crack on the Lakeview floor. I would like to note that this is very difficult, especially if you are trying to act like a normal sixth-grade girl and not like a complete freak, which I sometimes think I am.

I barely eat at lunch. Grace even offers me half of her tuna fish sandwich and I turn it down. My stomach is too busy practicing for the Ringling Brothers Circus for me to eat.

By seventh period I seriously consider making a trade deal with God. I decide to trade any remote chance that Ashton actually likes me back for the possibility of making the team. But just before the bell rings, I nix the deal. I want both.

When the bell finally rings after ninth period, I dart out of the room and run all the way to my locker. I fumble for a second with my combination lock, grab my backpack, jam my stuff in, and run outside.

In front of the school I wait by the pick-up zone, knowing Summer is coming to get me after she picks up Apple at her school first. I wait nervously until Summer and Apple finally pull up in their red Volvo. On the way to the rink, Summer gives us a big pep talk.

"Girls, no matter what happens, the important thing is that you went for it and tried!" she says. "And if you don't make it this year, you'll try again next year!"

But I don't want to get cut. I've never wanted something so badly in my life. Nobody can tell, but all the way to the rink I cross every finger on both hands. Just for luck.

As soon as Summer pulls in between the yellow lines of the parking space at the rink, Apple and I unbuckle our seat belts and jump out of the car. We race to the window next to the front entrance, where the list is hanging. Everything moves in slow motion. My heart is pounding.

"I can't look!" I say, covering my eyes with my hands.

"No, *you* have to look first!" Apple begs. We stand like this for two minutes, arguing back and forth about who should look and how we should do it, until we finally decide to both look at the exact same time.

"One, two, two and a half—" I say, dragging out the torture. "Three!"

I open my eyes and try to focus on the typed list. But Apple is ahead of me.

"Yes!" she shouts. "I made it! I made it!"

I am beginning to panic.

My stomach is churning.

My heart is pounding. I put my finger up to the list and slide it down, reading off every name, one by one.

```
Ithaca Comets 15U
Girls' Travel Team

Gendelman
Jensen
Erickson
McKenna
Goldsmith
Grossman
Sylvester
Robbins
Hughes
Wyatt
Johns
Dwyer
Grant
True
O'Shea
```

O'Shea!

O'Shea! O'Shea! O'Shea!

I gulp with relief. I am happy. Very happy. Blissfully happy.

Ice Cream

Apple and I float all the way back to the car. Summer walks between us with her arms draped around our shoulders, squeezing us. We are all very happy.

At the car Summer hands me her cell phone. "Call your dad, sweetheart. I am sure he will love to hear your good news!"

So I do. I call him at his lab on campus and tell him everything—the list, my name, Apple's name.

Finally he gets a word in. "That's great, Skye!" he says. "I knew you could do it, champ." He's proud of me. I can tell.

"Thanks," I say, smiling from ear to ear.

Summer decides we need to celebrate. We head straight to our favorite ice cream spot, Purity. Summer tells us to get anything our hearts desire. I boost myself up on the wooden step beneath the old-fashioned ice-cream counter and stare up at the board on the wall that lists the flavors. I don't really know why I do this because every time I come to Purity, I end up ordering the exact same thing—two scoops of cookies and cream with hot fudge, whipped cream, and rainbow sprinkles. Today is no different. Apple gets the same thing but with mocha chip ice cream. And even though it's kind of cold outside, we eat in front at the wooden picnic tables by the road. We try to get all the big trucks that pass by to honk.

When Summer and Apple drop me off in our driveway, I brace myself before walking up the back steps. I am pretty sure this is where my good day will end. My sisters don't get too excited about me, or anything that has to do with me, unless it's about me wearing their clothes without asking or something dumb like that. But when I walk through the door, the first thing I see is a yellow sign taped to the wall.

"WAY TO GO, SKYE #17! Ithaca Comets" is printed in marker in thick blue letters. My sisters both come running downstairs to greet me.

Shannon leaps over the back of the couch. "Way to go!" she says. "You're in the big time now, Skye!"

Shelby reaches under the sofa and pulls out a narrow box with shiny silver wrapping. "Here," she says.

I rip off the fancy paper, pry open the lid, and push aside the white tissue. Inside the box is my very own blue and gold Comets jacket. I shake it out, smoothing the wrinkles, and can't believe my eyes. "Skye" is stitched in script on the left chest. "17" is embroidered in thick gold numbers on the sleeve.

"You lucked out and even got your favorite number," Shannon says. "Coach Cosgrove told Dad when he saw him downtown."

"But I thought—"

"We all knew, Skye," Shannon tells me.

"Yeah, we knew all week, but Dad made us swear not to tell," Shelby explains.

I slip on my jacket and run upstairs to admire myself in my full-length mirror. My sisters both sit on my bed and watch me parade around my room.

"Don't get it dirty," Shelby teases.

"Yeah, try not to lose it," Shannon chimes in.

I get the feeling my sisters are kind of proud of me, but they don't really come out and actually say it.

For dinner, my mom cancels her last appointment at the hospital and we all pile into her blue minivan and head down the hill to meet my dad at Moosewood Restaurant. During dinner, everyone is in a good mood. There is not one fight the entire evening. At the round table in the middle of the crowded dining room, my sisters even give me a special toast.

"To Skye!" they say in unison, raising their glasses and smiling. We all lift our glasses and clink them together. I think this could very well be one of the best days of my life.

Rain on my Parade

I have three weeks until hockey practice officially starts, so for now my only exercise is gym. I change in the locker room. I mind my own business. Brooke Benton is changing at the locker next to mine.

"Skye, I have a question to ask you," she says, laughing. Brooke Benton is really tall and pretty but not so charming. The same goes for Brittany, her sidekick. "So, Skye, we were wondering—" Brooke bursts out laughing, as if there's some private joke going on that I am not clued in on. "We were wondering—" More laughing. "OK, we were wondering—" Long dramatic pause. "Why don't you shave your legs?" She blurts it out and thinks this is hilarious.

"Because that's nasty!" Brittany pipes in, looking at my legs, making a face like she is going to gag.

I smile, pretending to be in on their little joke, but really I don't know what else to do. I grab my jeans and slip them on quickly.

"No offense or anything, Skye, but we were just wondering," Brooke says again, putting her arm on my shoulder like she is just joking—even though she so obviously isn't. I honestly didn't think my legs looked bad at all until this very moment.

"You really might want to buy a razor!" Brittany says, still giggling.

I am completely embarrassed. And as I slip out the locker room door, I try to act cool and unfazed by this little incident. But truth be told, I am completely mortified.

Razor Sharp

As soon as I get home from school, I throw down my backpack and lock myself in the bathroom. First I run water in the bathtub, rinsing out remnants of Shelby's and Shannon's long red hair. Then I start filling the tub. I squirt in Shelby's green bubble bath for good measure, even though I know she will kill me if she ever finds out I touched it. Next I fold my school clothes into a neat pile on top of the toilet seat and step into the tub.

Resting my head on the back of the tub, I lie back into the warm water until the bubbles cover me. I think about how excited I am for hockey season to start. I think about Ashton, how cute he is, and the fact that I saw him three times today—once at lunch, once outside by the basketball courts, and once in science. And then, even though I don't exactly know what I'm doing and I know I should probably ask my mom first, I grab Shannon's purple plastic razor and rinse it out in the sudsy water. I stick my foot up on the faucet in front of me, squirt more of Shelby's green bubble bath on my shin, and lather up until my entire left leg is covered with white foamy bubbles.

I begin with my ankle and glide the razor carefully up to my knee. I do this all the way around my leg until I have shaved off all the white soap. One leg down. I switch legs and lather up again, wondering what the big deal is. This is right about the moment I feel a major sharp pain coming from the middle of my shin.

And if you get grossed out easily, stop reading here, because it gets disgusting. Blood is now gushing out of my skin, and dangling from the razor is a long, pink, narrow strip of my very own skin. I know, I know, I completely agree with you—it is disgusting. That is precisely why, at this very moment, I am feeling very sick. My shin throbbing in pain, I awkwardly lift myself out of the bath, grab a big wad of toilet paper, and hold it tightly against the cut to stop the bleeding. And then I just sit on the blue bath mat and cry. Why do girls have to shave their legs anyway?

I will wear sweatpants to gym from now on.

Three Days Later

I finish all my homework . . . well, all of it except for my idiotic math homework. Because I'm so stupid and can't do it, I need to get help tomorrow from the evil sorceress. I sit down at my mom's desk in her study and turn on the computer. Olivia, Grace, Jasmine Green, and Caitlyn are all online, so we instant message until everybody has to get off. Then I decide to try this cool people-finder thing that Isabel showed me. You just type in the name of the person you are trying to find and the city and state they live in, and press return. I type in my name first, just to see if anything comes up.

Name	Skye Beryl O'Shea
City	Ithaca, New York

Nothing. I try my mom.

Name	Dr. Gabrielle Goldstein-O'Shea
City	Ithaca, New York

Nothing. And I'm just about to give up when I remember the perfect person to try next. I run down the hall to my room and dump the contents of my blue backpack on the floor until I find my yellow language arts folder. I spread all the papers out onto the floor until I find what I am looking for—my Who I Admire paper.

Skye O'Shea

Language Arts

Ms. Hahn

Period 1

Who I Admire:
Haley Bryce
World's Greatest Hockey Player

Haley Bryce is one of the best women's ice hockey players in the world. She was born in Maple Grove, Minnesota. Haley started playing hockey when she was five years old. She has three older brothers and one younger sister and they all play hockey too. During the long Minnesota winters, they played hockey every day on a frozen pond in there) ! neighborhood.

When Haley was little, there were no girls' teams to play on so she played on all-boys' teams until she went to college. In high school she was on the Maple Grove High School team, which won the 1988 Minnesota State Championships. She was the first girl to play on an all-boys' team in the state of Minnesota. Her team voted her MVP and captain of the team.

After high school, Haley Bryce went to Brown University. After graduating from Brown in 1992, Haley was a teacher and girls' hockey coach in Massachusetts and trained for the national team. In 1998 Haley Bryce was on the first women's hockey team to play in the Olympics. The Olympics were in Nagano, Japan. In the Olympics the U.S.A. won the gold medal.

Besides playing hockey, Haley says two of her favorite things to do are "reading good books and canoeing." Her favorite book is <u>Maiden Voyage</u> by Tania Aebi, about a girl who sails by herself around the world. She also likes listening to music and playing the piano.

sources?

I admire Haley Bryce because she is a pioneer for women's ice hockey. She is probably one of the greatest women's hockey players to ever play the game. And she paved the way for girls like me. Plus we have the same number, 17!

Yes!

SKYE,
THIS IS REALLY
A WONDERFUL
JOB! A! :"

I run back to the study and place the paper next to me on my mom's desk.

Name	Haley Bryce
City	Maple Grove, Minnesota

I type carefully, cross my fingers, and press return. It takes about a minute, but it works.

I match found
1 of 1 items:

Haley Bryce
Rural Route 33
Maple Grove, MN 55311

"Awesome!" I say out loud, as I write down the address. I'm pretty sure this is the real Haley Bryce, because how many Haley Bryces can there be in Maple Grove, Minnesota? I turn off the computer, make sure everything is neat on my mom's desk so she doesn't freak, grab my Haley Bryce report, and head back to my room. Then I sit down at my messy desk and push all the paper off the top so there's a clean space to write.

Dear Haley,

My name is Skye O'Shea and I'm 11 years old. First of all, is this really you?!!! Because I found your address on the Internet. So I hope this is you! IF THIS IS NOT YOU, PLEASE DISREGARD THIS LETTER WHOEVER YOU ARE!!!

I play hockey too. I just made the Ithaca Comets 15U team! Our first real practice is this Thursday. I was wondering if you could PLEASE give me some tips on how to score a lot. (Since you're good at that ☺). Also, I was wondering if there's any other advice you could give me. I read that you have 3 brothers and 1 sister. My older sisters are identical twins, and they both play hockey too.

By the way, what's your middle name?

Well, I better get to bed. GOOD LUCK in hockey and with everything!! Please write me back!!!

I think you are the best hockey player in the world. And besides that, you are really cool. Also you were AWESOME in the Olympics. I watched every game. Thanks for reading this letter.

Yours Truly,

Skye #17

Skye Beryl O'Shea #17

P.S. I play center too.

P.P.S. Please Please Please Write Back Soon!!!

I lick the envelope shut with my tongue and stick a stamp on it. Before I can chicken out I run downstairs and right out the door in my pajamas. It's freezing and I have bare feet so I run as fast as I can to the mailbox, stick my letter in, and put the flag up so that the mailman will pick up the letter tomorrow.

I am an optimist. Mr. McDonnell told me that once in third grade. "You are always thinking positively, Skye. That's a good quality to have." At the bottom of my report card where the comments go, he wrote: "You are an optimist. Always stay that way."

I am almost positive Haley Bryce will write me back.

One Day Later

I don't know, maybe Mr. McDonnell was wrong. Maybe I'm not so optimistic.

From the desk of Jane Mitchell
Lakeview Middle School

Dear Gabrielle and Lance,

Skye is experiencing some difficulty and frustration with fractions and percents. She is also very hesitant to admit that she doesn't understand a lesson, which in turn builds her frustration. She would benefit from working on each day's lesson each night at home. I would be happy to discuss this further with you. I also have some names of math tutors from Cornell, which might be something to look into. Looking forward to speaking with you soon.

Sincerely,

Jane Mitchell
555-5547

"The only negative things in my room are numbers!"

As you can see, I am in deep math trouble.

Deep.

Very deep.

I am *so* depressed.

I hate school and I hate all my stupid teachers, except Ms. Hahn. And I'll hate my mom and dad if they don't let me go to hockey tomorrow. That would be totally and completely unfair! I've begged them since the first week of school to let me switch into the easier math class, but my dad just keeps giving me one of his top-ten favorite lines: "I know you can do it, Skye," or "Keep at it, Skye." I can't remember which.

When my mom gets home, I remove the note from the very bottom of my backpack where I have buried it, flatten it out on the dining room table, and hand it over to her in the kitchen. She reads it quickly and looks up at me.

"Maybe hockey will be too much to add to your first year of middle school, Skye," she says. She is totally serious. "We will sit down and discuss it tonight when your father gets home. For now you can do me a favor and start emptying the dishwasher."

Ugh!

Three Hours Later

When my parents call me into the living room, I am pretty sure my hockey future is about to go down the drain. The living room is really fancy and we use it only for two reasons: when company comes over or if my mom and dad want to lecture us. I sink into the big green puffy chair and face my parents, who are sitting across from me on the blue couch.

"Skye," my mom starts.

I'm already crying. I can't help it.

"Pull yourself together, Skye," my dad says, handing me a box of tissues. I blow my nose hard. "Look, we aren't going to say you can't play hockey."

My tears come to a screeching halt. I look up. My dad is still talking.

"What we do need from you is—" he stops. "Do you need to blow your nose?" I blow my nose again. "Skye, what we need from you is a commitment that you are going to see to it that you improve your math grade," he says.

I start nodding my head "yes," even though I have absolutely no idea how I am going to accomplish this feat. But I don't really care because all I really care about is that I can still play hockey.

Then my mom joins in. "Skye, I've spoken

with Mrs. Mitchell and we both agree you need a tutor."

I think I kind of roll my eyes. OK, I *do* roll my eyes. My mom does not like this gesture at all.

"Look, you need to be mature about this," she says. "You're not a baby anymore. If you expect to have the privileges of a young adult, then you need to show that you understand your priorities." I nod apologetically. I don't want my parents changing their minds about hockey. I give them my best, most sincere look.

"I've arranged for a tutor," my mom continues. "She's a Cornell student and she sounds very nice. You're meeting her downtown at the library, and that will happen every Wednesday until you feel more comfortable with math."

A math tutor? What? Did I hear this right? But nobody seems to really want to discuss this further, so I don't press it. It would not be a good idea, if you know what I mean. I am not happy, though. I do not like the idea of meeting some person I don't even know and having in-depth discussions about my absolutely least-favorite subject of all time.

My parents both get up and leave the room. There is no wrap-up discussion, no "You can do it, Skye," no "We believe in you, darling."

Uh-uh.

Nothing.

I pry myself out of the chair and walk into the kitchen. My notebooks are scattered across the kitchen table. I gather them all, jamming them one by one into my backpack, and head upstairs.

Don't get me wrong. I am totally, completely thankful and relieved that I get to play hockey. But I'm still in a very, very extremely bad mood.

First Practice

Lauren is standing at the door to the ice with a big roll of tape and a thick blue marker. She rips off a piece of white hockey tape, writes "Skye" on it in big blue letters, and sticks it on my helmet. She smoothes out the tape and winks at me. "Let's see what ya got, O'Shea!"

I step out onto the ice smiling. I'm not really that nervous anymore. As soon as everyone is on the ice, Coach Cosgrove blows his whistle and raises his stick above his head, signaling for us to huddle up. We skate to center ice. Lauren stands in front of us, next to Coach Cosgrove.

"All right, girls. Welcome to day one!" Lauren says.

"Are you ready?" Coach Cosgrove asks.

"*Yeah!*" we shout back. It's cool to see our team all together for the first time, everyone wearing matching gold helmets, blue and gold practice jerseys, and solid blue socks.

Coach Cosgrove jumps right into the first drill. "Circle drill," he says. "Let's hustle!"

Everyone races to the far corner of the ice and lines up along the boards. Logan is first. We skate around all five circles painted on the ice. I like this drill. It's easy. Plus, crossovers happen to be one of my specialties.

"Awesome!" Lauren says to me as I whiz by.

Coach Cosgrove blows the whistle and shouts, "Star drill!" And since I have no clue what the star drill is, I decide to follow Cash Erickson to the end of the line. Coach Cosgrove is standing in front of us.

"I'll explain this once," he says. "If you don't understand, watch and ask."

I have no idea what we are doing and, to be honest, I have this bad habit of tuning out during directions. So when Coach Cosgrove says, "Skye O'Shea, why don't you start us off?" I almost faint. I have absolutely no clue what we are supposed to do.

I skate forward to the front of the line, ahead of Logan. Why did he pick me, of all people? My heart is beating really loud and fast, and I feel like I'm going to pass out from complete embarrassment.

Everybody is watching. Then a voice magically speaks up behind me.

It's Logan. I turn my head just a tiny bit so I can hear her. "Just skate out to around the point and get ready for a pass from Coach," she tells me in a low whisper. "Then shoot on net." I decide right then and there to vote for Logan for captain.

During the rest of the practice we hardly touch the pucks. We just skate and skate until it feels like my legs may completely fall off.

After practice we are all sweaty and worn out. We're taking off our skates in the locker room when Coach Cosgrove and Lauren come in.

"If for any reason you cannot make a practice, I expect you to call me," Coach Cosgrove says. "You are on a select travel team. This team should be one of your top priorities, right behind your family and school." He finishes his speech, looks over at Lauren, and nods.

She continues. "You have been chosen for your hockey skills and for the way you carry yourselves. We expect you to be a class act—in school and on the ice." They both look around the room slowly, smiling at the team. Then they turn around and walk out.

For a couple of seconds everyone is totally quiet. Then Logan makes a snowball from the ice on her skate and throws it at Rachel. Everyone gets into this big ice- and tape-ball fight, until Logan shouts above the noise.

"All right, you guys!" she yells. Nobody hears her. "*Shut up!*" she yells louder. Then she whistles *really* loud, finally getting everyone's attention. Logan steps up on the wooden bench with her skates still on. "Tomorrow's Team Spirit Day," she announces. "Everybody wear your blue jersey and your pajama bottoms to school."

"Awesome!" says Sidney.

"Cool!" Cash shouts. "I love team spirit."
Everybody seems excited.

Everybody, that is, except Abigail Dwyer.
I've really only known her for one day, but I can
tell she's not the most positive person on earth.
She is sitting in the corner by the garbage pail.

"You guys," Abigail whines, "I will not wear
pajama bottoms to school. That is so *stupid!*"

For a split second, nobody says a thing.

Logan glances up from untying her skates.
"Fine," she says, smiling. "You don't have to, but
everybody else is!"

Abigail lets out this big "Whatever!" She
throws her stuff into her bag and pouts out the
door. Nobody really pays any attention to her
anyway. She's always in a bad mood.

I will sleep well tonight. I will sleep so well
and so deeply that I will not even dream. I am
so, so, *so* tired. But it's the good kind of tired.
I have survived my first practice. I love hockey.

Team Spirit

Just as we planned last night on the phone, Isabel meets me on my back porch at 6:50. We quietly sneak up into the bathroom before my sisters are even stirring. Isabel brings the special black hairbrush her mom got her from Japan, plus two hair ties and her blue plaid pajama bottoms. I run to my room and change out of my plain gray sweatpants and into Isabel's plaid pj's. They fit me perfectly. I slip my blue and gold Comets jersey over my head and take a quick look in the full-length mirror on my closet door, admiring myself before I run back to the bathroom for our hair project. I put the lid down on the toilet and sit facing Isabel, who quickly goes to work brushing out my thick brown hair, dividing it neatly into sections.

Isabel braids my hair into six different rows in the front and pulls the rest back into a pony-tail. As soon as she's finished, she lets me sneak a peek in the mirror, but then we have to rush so we won't miss the bus. I wolf down a bagel and gulp some orange juice. We both grab our backpacks and run all the way to Kyle Kimber's brick driveway.

Everybody loves my hair. "Cute!" Paige says when I sit down next to her on the bus.

"You're so lucky to have Isabel as your

neighbor," Olivia says enviously. It's true. I'm totally lucky. Even I have to admit that my hair looks really cool. My jersey is a hit, too. In front of our entire homeroom, Ms. Hahn asks me when our first game is. I am kind of embarrassed and kind of not, because I sort of feel like a celebrity.

At the end of school, Paige is waiting for me at my locker. I throw everything in my bag: science, social studies, language arts, and math. I'm in such a rush to leave that I almost don't notice the small, tightly folded note that is jammed in the vent of my locker door. I glance around to see who is watching. Paige is busy flirting with Cole Olson, whose locker is next to mine. The note is folded into a compact little triangle and wedged tight into the vent. I tug it slowly, being careful not to rip it on the sharp edges of the metal locker.

"FOR SKYE O'SHEA #17" is written neatly in black marker on the face of the triangle.

I begin to have major heart palpitations.

I have never gotten a note before, unless you count the notes Paige sends to tell me how bored she is in study hall. I have a feeling this note might be something different.

It looks like boy writing.

I turn and glance over at Paige and Cole. I quickly decide to open my mysterious note in the privacy of my very own room. I drop the note safely into the top pocket of my backpack and zip the pocket shut.

The Note

On the bus ride home, it feels as if the note is burning a hole right through my backpack. *Who could it be from?* I wonder, staring out the window. I am having a hard time paying attention to Paige, who is explaining the social studies homework we both have to do. I stare at my bag on the grimy bus floor and seriously consider opening the note right this second. But I decide I'd better wait—I mean, just to be on the safe side.

When the bus drops me off, I do a quick look for Isabel, but she's not there. So I run all the way home without stopping. When I get to the back door, I'm still breathing heavily from my 200-yard dash from the bus. Once inside, I don't even take off my shoes like I'm supposed to or dump my backpack at the closet door. Instead I bound up the stairs to my room.

My room is a disaster area, exactly how I left it this morning. I shut the door and lock it and throw my backpack down next to my night table. I plop down on my unmade bed, reach into my backpack, and pull out the note. Carefully, I unfold it and smooth it out on my mattress.

Skye,
You sort of know me
and you sort of don't.
I think you are really
cool and I would really,
really like to go out with
you.
     Good luck in hockey!
Love,
A guy you're just friends with
who wants to be more.

I am frozen on top of my bed, my heart beating fast and loud. Is this somebody's idea of a joke? Do I really have a secret admirer? I think about these two options and really hope it is the second one. I mean, maybe somebody really does *like* me. I am smiling. A half dozen Lakeview sixth-grade boys flash in front of my eyes, their faces displayed before me like a slide show. Tyler from homeroom? He always kind of stares at me funny. Xavier from science? No, he likes Caitlyn. Maybe it's Cole Olson—his locker's next to mine and he always talks to me about hockey, but I'm positive he likes Paige. No matter who I picture or who I think it might be, I keep coming back to the same single wish and the same single face.

Ashton.

One side of me thinks I should not even

consider this an option. I mean, maybe I'm setting myself up for a major disappointment. Because, well, it would be just too perfect for the one boy in the entire school who I actually like to like me back. But then the other side of me thinks maybe, just maybe, it's Ashton.

"Please!" I close my eyes tightly and pray. "Please, please, please, just this once, let it be him."

One Week Later

I am sitting in the cafeteria with my usual crowd when Paige announces we are going outside by the basketball court. It's sunny and warm, and we have a lot of Halloween candy to demolish before the bell rings. I peel the rubbery orange cheese off my bagel and roll it into a little ball. Once again, I have forgotten to bring my lunch and I'm paying for it big time. When I walk over to dump my plate in the garbage, I feel someone's hot breath on my ear.

I flinch and turn to look. It's Nate Tanner.

"Hey, Skye, I've got to tell you something," he says, standing about two inches away from me. I can feel spit inside my eardrum. Gross.

Nate Tanner is at least one foot shorter than I am. He has pale peach skin with freckles covering his nose and cheeks. His hair is straw blond, thick, and straight.

He is staring at me.

I am staring back.

Neither of us says anything.

I am thinking he isn't really my type. Too short. Too shy. Too not my type. I look down at him. "Sorry about that," he says nervously, apologizing for the whole breath-in-the-ear thing. I smile as nicely as I can and wait for him to say whatever it is he wants to say. I am being polite, but I would be lying if I don't admit the other major lightbulb moment I am having here.

Nate Tanner happens to be Ashton's best friend.

They're always together. They are both on the wrestling team and they eat lunch at the same table, with all the other athletic guys in my grade. My overactive imagination goes wild.

I am picturing Ashton sending a message to me through Nate. I am picturing walking hand in hand with Ashton. I am picturing us officially going out. And I don't really know what any of this looks like, but I'm picturing it just the same. I mean, what else would Nate Tanner want?

"Ummm . . ." Nate is having a hard time getting out whatever he has to say. "Ummm," he says again.

I am beginning to have compassion for Nate Tanner. I give him my best it's-OK-I-know-what-you-are-going-to-tell-me-so-you-don't-even-have-to-say-it look. Because, after all, it's so obvious what this is about.

He looks over my shoulder at the boys' bathroom door. "I just want to tell you . . . um, well, the thing is . . ."

My heart starts to thump so loud, I'm sure Nate can hear it. *Tell me! Tell me! Tell me!* I think to myself.

He moves his eyes from the door to the ground and continues. "The thing is, I know someone who really likes you." He makes a big point of emphasizing "someone."

I am trying to act cool and calm, but I'm really ready to jump up and down. I mean, he doesn't actually say Ashton's name, but it's *obvious!*

I do not make it outside to share the news or everyone's Halloween candy, but I don't really care about candy. I float to fifth period, half watching where I'm going through the crowded hallway, half thinking about the odds that Nate's "someone who likes me" is actually Ashton. By ninth period I decide my chances are seventy percent that it's Ashton, thirty percent that it's somebody else. I'm not that good at math, but really, who else can it be?

By the time I get my backpack and head outside to the bus, I think I will burst if I don't get to tell someone soon. It's enough that I haven't even told anyone about the note. I mean, I can't keep this big a secret any longer. So, slumping down in the green vinyl bus seat between Isabel and Paige, I decide to just tell them—about the notebook incident, the note, Nate whispering in my ear—*everything.*

"Wow!" Isabel says, smiling, her eyes open

wide, her eyebrows raised. "I've never had a secret admirer!" She says this just to make me feel special. We both know it's not true. The entire school is in love with Isabel, and she's going out with this really cute guy, Sam, the star of the fall play.

"I think it's Ashton Fergesen," says Paige. She seems so certain.

I am happy.

I am blushing.

I am hoping, majorly hoping, that she is right.

"Let's face it, Skye," says Paige. I put my finger up to my lips to remind her to keep it down. "Who else can it be?" she whispers.

We talk about it until Isabel and I get off the bus, and then Isabel and I talk about it even more until we part ways at the ends of both our driveways. I am very excited. I am practically floating. This is so cool. Nothing of this fabulous nature has happened to me before. This is the kind of thing I see in movies.

How It Works

Two days after what I will now refer to as "the secret note incident," Paige gives me some very valuable information. We are sitting on the bus, third seat back, and I am in the window seat. Paige is sitting next to me, leaning in from the aisle so nobody else can hear. We are on our way to school. Paige is explaining it all to me—the "going out" thing, I mean.

"I can't believe your sisters don't tell you this stuff," she says. Paige has this really cool older sister, Vanessa, who tells her absolutely everything. That's why Paige is way more advanced than I am when it comes to romance. Plus Paige has already had three boyfriends and it's only the third month of school.

"First of all," says Paige, "the number-one thing to remember is that if you like somebody or if somebody likes you, you don't have to go up and tell him face-to-face. That's just not how you do it."

I look at her, kind of confused.

"What you do is—" Paige notices she is talking kind of loud and adjusts her voice to a whisper. "OK, what you do is find somebody who will go up and ask the guy you like out *for* you. Or the guy that likes you gets a friend to ask you if you like him. Then that friend goes back and tells the guy what you said," Paige says, smiling.

I sit in homeroom and can't think of anything but this new information Paige has provided. I think of Ashton and wonder who I would choose to have talk to him for me—even though I never actually would do that because it would be way too embarrassing. But if I was going to do it, I'd probably ask Paige to help, because she has this mystical effect on boys that causes them to melt, stare, and do anything she says. And just in case you don't believe me about that, in fourth period Jacob Riley comes up to me at the end of chorus. We are standing around waiting to be dismissed.

"Hey, Skye," Jacob says. I look up kind of surprised because, well, to be honest, Jacob Riley is pretty hot. "You're really tight with Paige, right?" he asks. He seems kind of nervous.

"Yeah," I nod, and smile. I am a little at a loss for words.

"Would you tell her I like her?" he asks.

Jacob Riley is majorly cute. I can't believe he is talking to me, or that he even actually knows my name. I nod, mesmerized by his dark eyes, dark brown skin, and perfect teeth.

"And ask her if she likes me back," he says, his smile sparkling. "Ask her if she'll go out with me."

At lunch I wait until I can talk to Paige alone. Finally, outside the cafeteria, I tell her the message word for word. Paige is very happy. Jacob Riley is ultra popular and cute. Paige is forgetting for the time being that she is really in love with Cole Olson.

I go back inside the cafeteria and find Jacob. I tell him Paige has accepted his offer. This is all it takes. Jacob and Paige are officially "going out."

Two Weeks Later

I am clearing the table after dinner, stacking the plates on the counter next to the sink. My mom is rinsing off the plates and loading the dishwasher when she turns toward me and begins the conversation I've been dreading.

"Skye, remember that tomorrow you are meeting your tutor right after school at the library." I roll my eyes without even trying to. I have been seriously hoping my parents had forgotten about this plan. "Listen," she says, lecturing me for the zillionth time, "you need to keep an open mind. This girl might surprise you. She sounds very pleasant on the phone."

"But I don't even know her," I start.

"Skye, you're wasting your breath," she says. "You don't really have any choice in this matter, sweetheart. End of conversation."

Considering my first game is this weekend, I opt to not rock the boat, and I walk away, grudgingly accepting my fate.

Lucky Me

I am bummed the entire day of school. I do not want to just go meet some girl I don't even know. What if she's weird or something?

I am not happy. I am mad at my parents. I am mad at Mrs. Mitchell. This is not fair! How can they do this to me?

And to top it all off, I am not looking forward to walking all the way to the library, which is at least a mile from school. But I really don't have any choice. So when the bell rings at the end of ninth period, I head straight to my locker and grab my folders and books. I throw them in my backpack, slip on my blue hockey jacket, and start the long walk alone.

I am almost over the bridge right past the high school when I hear someone running up behind me. I look back over my shoulder to see who it is.

No way.

No way! I think I am imagining this. I think my brain is playing tricks on me. Quickly turning my head, I check one more time with the same results. My heart starts pounding.

Be cool.

Breathe.

Stay calm.

His footsteps get closer and closer until

Ashton is right there beside me. My stomach starts to churn. But by some complete miracle, I manage to compose myself and smile. "Hey," I say in the best cool, casual voice I can muster.

"Hey, I've been trying to catch up with you since the tennis courts," Ashton says. "You walk fast!" We both laugh nervously. His blond hair is sticking out of his tattered red baseball cap. He's breathing pretty hard, out of breath from running.

"Where are you going?" I manage to blurt out. "I mean, don't you have wrestling?" I am hoping I don't sound as totally nerdy as I feel at this very moment.

Ashton walks next to me, practically brushing up against me with his green backpack. "Oh, no. I can't wrestle until my cast is off. But Wednesdays after school I have to meet my tutor in the library. I've had one since my accident, ya know, to help me get caught up and stuff," he replies, smiling.

"Every Wednesday?" I ask, not believing my complete and absolute luck. He nods.

I say a special thank-you prayer. But not out loud—I am not that nerdy. He asks me where I'm going. I think about skipping the math-tutor part and saying I'm just walking downtown, but before I know it, it all comes spilling out of me.

I tell him about Mrs. Mitchell and my tutor and how much I hate math.

"Yeah, math stinks. You should switch to Mr. Valasquez. He's really nice and it's not that hard, either," he says.

And this is when I try desperately to think of something smart, cute, and funny to say. But all that comes out is "I know."

Even though the walk from Lakeview to the library takes twenty minutes, it seems like we are there in two seconds. Ashton and I stand across the street from the library, waiting for the light to change. I am hoping he will say something like "Skye, did you get my note? Do you want to go out with me?" or "Skye, you are so beautiful. I can't keep my eyes off you!" But this does not take place. Instead, he pulls a thick black marker out of his pocket, rolls up the sleeve of his jacket, and asks me to sign his cast. Then he holds his arm perfectly still while I write as neatly as I can—in the only little blank space I can find, by his elbow—"Get well soon! Skye #17."

Kiesha

As soon as we walk through the front door of the library, Ashton turns to me and waves with his good hand. He bounds up the stairs to meet his tutor, a tall guy with an orange beard. I'm so charmed by my recent good luck that I almost forget why I'm even at the library. I stand in a daze by the water fountain for a few seconds, and then a really tall girl walks up.

"Skye?" she asks.

"That's me." I nod, look up at her, and smile politely.

"Well, hey, my name's Kiesha. I'm your tutor," she says.

She is majorly tall. I mean *really* tall. And she does not look like the weird, crazy, yucky person I imagined I'd be stuck with. I follow her to the big round tables way in the back of the library by the oversized books. She is wearing a red sweatshirt with "Cornell Volleyball" written across the back. We sit down at the table in the farthest corner of the room. She has these cool, long, thin braids in her hair, and they're really pretty. She tells me she's an engineering major. She wants to design suspension bridges and stuff like that. She asks me about hockey, which I think is very nice of her. She tells me about volleyball— she started playing when she was seven years old.

And then we get to work.

After an entire hour of math, for the first time in my life my brain doesn't hurt while thinking about fractions. I actually get it. I am even smiling. Well, almost smiling. I mean, if you can smile when it comes to math, then I am smiling.

"There is hope for you, Skye!" Kiesha jokes. "You are smart. You can do this." She looks me in the eye. "You just have to start believing in yourself, Skye."

And I don't mean to be rude or anything, but Kiesha is a million times smarter than Mrs. Mitchell is. I mean, if Mrs. Mitchell had explained this stuff to me like Kiesha did, I would have totally gotten it from the beginning.

After Kiesha leaves, I still have a half hour before my dad is picking me up. I pack up my backpack and explore the library. I pretend to be looking for books, but really I am hoping to run into a certain someone. But there is no sign anywhere of Ashton or the guy with the orange beard. So I head outside, zip up my hockey jacket, and sit down on the green wooden bench next to the curb in front of the library. I am waiting for my dad. It is freezing, snow is falling fast, and the wind is blowing. My nose is so cold,

I think it might fall off. Dad's blue truck finally pulls up. And even though I am frozen solid, my teeth are chattering, and my fingers are numb, I don't really mind.

"How was your day, champ?" he asks, looking over at me.

And all I can do is smile.

Game Day

The one-hour drive to the Syracuse rink seems long, and it's so early in the morning that it's still dark. The only light that shines comes from the entrance to the arena. Summer drops us off at the door and Apple and I follow the arrows on the wall, lugging our bags down a long, dark hallway until we find our locker room. As soon as I push open the heavy metal door, I practically gag. The entire locker room smells gross, as if the toilet has overflowed or something.

Logan is the only one in the locker room. She sits in the corner, tightening her skates. "Hey, I advise you guys to get dressed and out of here fast so you don't suffocate!" she says, making a face and plugging her nose.

It is really gross, and for a split second it occurs to me that this is a very bad omen for my first game as a Comet. I walk over to the garbage pail in the middle of the room and remove a broken wooden hockey stick. I take it out and prop it between the door and the wall so that the door stays open. This doesn't really help, but it creates an illusion of fresh air.

We dress quickly and meet the rest of our team by the Zamboni door. Once out on the ice, we warm up together until Lauren shouts, "Star drill!" This time I know just what to do. When the buzzer sounds, we all skate around our end really fast until Logan calls us over to our box.

I skate over to the rest of my teammates, packed tight in a huddle. I scrunch between Emma Grossman and Apple, our arms draped around each other in a giant hug. We all look up at Coach Cosgrove, who's standing on the bench. "Girls, you've practiced hard," he says. "Now go out there and skate hard—and have fun!"

Everyone is fired up. We all crowd close together, our hands piled up one on top of another in one big lump in the middle.

"All right, on three," Logan says. "One, two, three!" And on three we shout in unison, "GO, COMETS!"

I'm centering the third line, so I sit down on the bench, squeezing between my line mates, Cleo Grant on left wing and Tessa True on right. By the second period our team is ahead by one goal, 2-1. Logan scores the first goal and Cash gets the second.

"Hey, we're up next!" Cleo says, nudging me with her elbow, motioning me to line up next to the door. At the next whistle we head out.

"You're doing great, Skye. Way to hustle!" Lauren says, tapping me lightly on the top of my gold helmet as I walk past her and step onto the ice. Just like I've practiced in my driveway with my sisters a thousand times, I win the face-off and pass the puck back to Jamie on defense. Only Jamie isn't expecting my pass. The puck flies past her and heads straight toward our goal. I chase after the gold Syracuse jersey in front of me.

I can almost touch her.

She's one step away—

"Go, Skye!" my teammates yell.

"You can do it, Skye!" shouts a parent from the stands.

"Get back! Get back!" I can hear Coach Cosgrove yelling from the bench.

Right then and there, I make a split-second decision. I dive through the air, my stick swinging out on the ice in front of me, trying to hit the puck away.

BAM! My head hits the ice hard. I am sliding across the ice smack on top of the Syracuse player, sailing right toward Rachel in goal.

"Get off me!" shouts the girl from Syracuse, pushing me with her glove. But I can't get off her. The blade of my skate is somehow caught on her stick. We are sliding together straight for the net.

And the next thing I know, Syracuse girl and I are lying in a heap inside the net.

A handful of gold-jerseyed Syracuse players are leaping up and down and jumping on each other in front of me. This is just about the time it hits me: I slid right on top of the puck and carried it with me, past Rachel, into our own goal! *I scored on my own team!* This is so *not* how I have pictured my first goal as a Comet. I struggle to get up, but I'm stuck beneath the Syracuse girl who is sitting on top of me.

She untangles her stick from my skate and gets up. "Nice goal, loser!" she says, looking down at me and grinning evilly. I look up at Rachel.

"Sorry about that," I mumble, humiliated. Cash skates up to the goal and reaches out her hand, pulling me up from the inside of the net. "Don't worry about it, Skye," she says, patting me on the back. "We'll get them back." And I can't tell you how much I really, really, *really* want to believe her.

Shake It Off

"Shake it off, Skye!" Lauren says, patting the top of my helmet as I climb over the boards and slump onto the bench. I feel like a complete idiot. I have just managed to score my very first career goal as a Comet, and I scored it on my own goalie! To say that I feel stupid is an understatement. If it wasn't me, I would probably laugh, because it's almost funny. But it *is* me and it isn't funny—at all.

We stay on the bench between periods. Coach Cosgrove takes out his dry-erase board and red marker and draws a rink. He diagrams the way he wants us to throw the puck up the boards to help us break out of the defensive zone quicker. "I want to see a blue jersey every time I see the puck," he says. "I want to see you hustle! And for goodness' sake, *shoot* the puck!"

Lauren nods in agreement. "Come on, girls. Let's go out there and play like I know we can play!" she says. The buzzer sounds.

My head is reeling. I can't get my stupid goal out of my mind. I try to concentrate on the game. I try to think of the third period. I stick my arm into the middle of the huddle.

"OK, Comets. On three!" says Logan. "One, two, three!"

"GO, COMETS!" we shout.

For most of the third period we race up and down the ice, both teams shooting on net, but nobody scores. With two minutes left in the game, the score is still tied 2-2. Everybody on the bench is screaming, including me. We are banging our sticks against the boards. "*Let's go, blue! Let's go, blue!*" we chant together.

My heart is racing. And for the first time in my life, I am glad I am not on the ice. I am too nervous, and I do not want to lose. There are thirty-three seconds left in the game when Coach Cosgrove sends our five strongest players onto the ice. Logan, Cash, Anna Sylvester, Sidney Johns, and Madison Gendelman line up for a face-off in front of the Syracuse goal. The tension is mounting. Everyone is standing up.

"You can do it, Comets!" the parents shout.

"Let's go, Logan!" screams Jamie Hughes from the bench.

"Let's go, Comets!" screeches Apple at the top of her lungs.

Logan wins the face-off and passes a perfect drop pass back to Cash. We all watch Cash's slap shot from the point, almost as if it's in slow motion. It is a hard shot—a high shot. And just before the buzzer, the puck sneaks past the Syracuse goalie and into the upper right-hand corner of the net!

I jump over the boards and join the rest
of my team in celebration. We pile on top of Cash
in front of the goal. For a good minute
or two, I completely forget the fact that, in
my debut game as a Comet, I have scored on my
very own goalie.

One Day Later

I am eating breakfast at the kitchen table, minding my own business, when Shannon says it to me. "I heard you scored a goal yesterday!"

I roll my eyes, and even though Mom is at work, I hear her voice in my head: *Just ignore them, Skye. Don't let them bring you down to their level.* I turn away from Shannon and concentrate on my cereal. I haven't seen my sisters since Friday night because they were at a tournament in Ottawa with my dad.

Apparently this morning is Pick on Skye Day. My sisters are laughing hysterically. "Do you think—" Shelby has trouble speaking because she's laughing so hard. "Do you think you'll get in the paper for that one?" She thinks this is hilarious.

"Yeah, Skye O'Shea notched one for Syracuse Sunday!" adds Shannon.

Ha ha ha. They think they are so funny. I do not. I sit, wishing my dad would magically appear and send them both to their rooms, yell at them, or do something to punish them. But he has already left for work. So naturally, I do the only thing I can think of. I reach over and punch Shannon on her arm as hard as I can.

My sister does not like this. I have surprised her. "Ow! You stupid little brat!" she shouts. But

I am one step ahead of her. And before she can hit me back, strangle me, or pinch me, I grab my backpack and run outside, slamming the door behind me.

On my way to the bus, I wipe my eyes and hope nobody will notice that I have been crying. Kyle Kimber looks at me a little funny, but other than that, I don't think anyone notices. At least no one says anything to me—not even Isabel.

After school my sisters are home, and they act like nothing even happened. Shannon doesn't apologize or anything. So I barricade myself in my room and do my homework until dinner.

You've Got Mail

After dinner I sit at my desk. I am in a terrible mood. This has not been a good day. To make matters worse, I am attempting my stupid math homework. I hear a knock on my door.

"WHAT?" I shout in a not-very-nice tone of voice.

"Skye?" It's my mom.

"I'm doing homework," I say, hoping everybody will just leave me alone.

"OK, but I think I have something here that will cheer you up, sweetheart," she says. She opens the door a crack, tosses a big, thick envelope on my desk, smiles at me, and leaves, gently shutting the door behind her.

I pick up the envelope and examine it carefully. Across the center in neat red handwriting is my name—Ms. Skye Beryl O'Shea #17—and address. Three colorful hockey stamps adorn the top right-hand corner.

Hockey stamps? Hockey stamps!

"Oh my gosh, oh my gosh, oh my gosh!" I say it over and over again in total shock. "YES!" I scream, so loud that I'm sure my entire family can hear me.

My mom has apparently told my sisters about my good fortune, because they have barged into my room and are standing in the doorway.

"OPEN IT! OPEN IT!" they shout together, as if suddenly they are my best friends. "Here, let me do it for you," Shannon says, reaching out to grab the envelope from me. But before she can snatch it away, I slip between them and run into the bathroom, locking the door behind me.

I sit down on the cold tile floor, lean my back up against the bathtub, and open the top of the envelope, being careful not to rip anything. The first thing I see is an autographed picture of Haley Bryce. And then I see the note.

Haley Bryce 17
HaleyBryce17@aol.com

Dear Skye—
Thanks for your AWESOME letter! I hope you have a GREAT season in HOCKEY and in SCHOOL. Good luck! Remember, skate hard, hustle, and have fun!
Your friend, Haley #17

"You miss 100% of the shots you don't take."
Wayne Gretzky

My sisters are banging on the door. "Don't be a baby, Skye. Open the door!" Shannon says.

"Come on, Skye. Let us see it!" begs Shelby. She is pounding on the door. "Let us see! Come on, Skye, open up!"

But I don't move. I just sit there on the floor and stare at the note and the picture. Haley Bryce! *The* Haley Bryce, the most famous women's hockey player ever, has written to me! As soon as I open the bathroom door, my sisters rush in. Shannon snatches the envelope out of my hands and holds it high above my head where I can't reach it. "Give it back!" I demand. But it's too late. They are both standing in the bathroom staring at the letter and the picture. Their jaws have dropped.

"You so lucked out, Skye!" says Shelby.

"I can't believe she actually wrote to you," says Shannon. By this time my mom and dad are standing in the bathroom, too. We are all crowded around staring at the letter, which is now safely back in my hands. Everyone is impressed with my feat.

My dad puts his arm around me. "Skye," he says, "you must have written a very nice letter to get a beautiful response like that."

And even though it's getting late and I still have three chapters of reading to do, I ask my mom if I may please use her computer to e-mail Haley. She says that even though I still have homework, I can do it just this once. "After all, it's not every day you get mail from an Olympic champion!" she says, smiling and looking kind of proud of me.

I read the e-mail over a couple of times and click "Send" before I can change anything.

🖥 Thanks!			
🖳 Send	💾 Save	🗑 Delete	📎 Add Attachments

From: **Skye17hockey**

To: **HaleyBryce17**

Subject: Thanks!

▷ Attachments: *none*

Dear Haley,

Thanks for your letter and the picture! I was really happy I got it today because, well, first of all because I am your biggest fan. But second of all, this weekend, in my very first game as a Comet, I scored on my own team! We still won 3-2 but it was completely embarrassing.

Well, I'd better get back to finishing my homework. Did you like school? I don't. I am not too good at math and science but I am good at social studies, language arts, gym, chorus, and art. Good luck. I hope you win!

Your biggest fan,
Yours truly,

Skye Beryl O'Shea #17

P.S. Please write back as soon as you can!

Two Days Later

Ashton is not in school today. In science Justin Sullivan tells Mr. Hanson that Ashton has the flu. So I trudge to my locker, throw my stuff into my bag, and walk the entire distance to the library by myself. The walk seems a lot longer this time—without somebody to talk to, I mean.

When I finally get to the library, Kiesha is waiting for me in the back at the big round table, just as she told me she'd be. Ever since I met Kiesha, I've gotten two "checks" in a row on homework. I have not gotten a "check plus," though, because the evil sorceress is supremely picky and says I need to show my steps better.

Later, at hockey, nobody says anything about my stupid goal. It's almost like it never even happened. But it did. And to make up for it, I get ready really fast and am out on the ice before anyone else. Alone on the ice, I dump the entire bucket of pucks out in front of the net and start shooting. Last night in the bathtub, I made an oath to myself to take fifty shots before every practice. I am just winding up for shot number forty-seven when Coach Cosgrove blows the whistle for warm-ups. I might just get good at this.

Crash Into Me

He's back. I am getting my stuff at my locker, and Paige is waiting next to me. We are talking about Paige's French test, my global studies assignment, and the fact that we have way too much homework. One second we are standing there perfectly normal, and the next thing I know my math book and my global studies folder are knocked out of my clutches.

Great, just great, I think, watching helplessly as my papers flutter to the floor. Annoyed, I turn to look at whoever found it necessary to bump into *me* when there is a lot of unoccupied real estate in this hallway to walk through. But when I see the culprit, my face turns beet red, and I become more embarrassed than anything else.

"Sorry about that!" Ashton says, smiling up at me, gathering my papers from the floor and handing them back to me in a neat pile, my math book on top.

He is cute. Very cute. I smile. He smiles. I seem to have lost my ability to speak.

"Ahhh . . ." I try to get something out. "Thanks." I guess this is better than nothing.

"Sorry, Skye!" he says, walking backward, smiling. "See you next Wednesday," he shouts as he waves. He turns to run and catch up with the big group of boys he had been walking with.

Paige is my witness. "Boys have a very funny way of displaying affection," she says, smiling. I am smiling too.

"The locker crash incident," as I will now refer to it, is funny and weird and my stomach is doing backflips. Paige and I sit down in the back of the bus. "Trust me, Skye," she tells me, "the note's from him. I know it."

I guess time will tell, but I really wish it would tell me soon.

Six Days Later

I stay after in social studies because Mr. Thompson is taking a zillion years to pass out these worksheets. I can't just leave without one because they're due tomorrow. I stand in line impatiently, tapping my foot and glancing at the clock every two seconds. I know that if this takes much longer, I will miss my only chance to walk to the library with Ashton. I slowly make my way toward the front of the line, grab the worksheet from Mr. Thompson, and run as fast as I can for my locker. I practically collide with Ms. Miller in the stairwell. "Sorry!" I shout, and keep running.

"Excuse me!" she says, yelling after me. "You need to walk, young lady!" I throw on the brakes, round the corner to the sixth-grade wing, and spot Ashton at the end of the long hallway. He is standing right at my locker. There is major butterfly action in my stomach. I duck behind the entrance to the cafeteria. *What is he doing at my locker? Is he waiting for me?* And right then, I completely lose all my nerve. It's as if it evaporates right out of my body or sinks to my feet. And so I just freeze, hiding behind the corner until I can see that Ashton is gone.

I am such a chicken! I am so all talk, no action.

Shoot, shoot, shoot! Why'd I do that? Maybe

I can still catch up with him. Yes—I will catch up with him! I sprint full speed for my locker. I will grab my bag and catch up with him by the tennis courts.

I open my locker, grab my backpack, toss everything into it, and almost don't notice the tightly folded piece of white notebook paper jammed in the same place as the last note—in the vent of the metal locker door.

Tha-thump, tha-thump, tha-thump . . . There's a difference between an out-of-breath kind of heartbeat and a seeing-a-cute-guy kind of heartbeat. I am having both at the same time. My stomach is fluttering. He was right there at my locker!

It has to be him. It has to be him. I grab the note, slam my locker door shut, and throw on my jacket, all in one motion. One side of me knows that if I want to walk with Ashton, I'll have to run to catch up with him, but the other side of me is dying to read the note. I look around, confirming that I am alone in the empty hallway. I stop walking at the door to the guidance office and carefully unfold the note.

What's up S.k.y.e ?
I'm still thinking about
you a lot! Do you ever go
to the Lakeview Dances?
Are you going this week?
I hope I see you there!!
Love,
A guy who you're just
friends with, who wants to
be more ☺

My face, already red, now turns completely hot and sweaty. He was *right there*—right by my locker. It has to be Ashton! I think about this as I start an all-out sprint toward the tennis courts. Maybe he'll finally say something about it to me today.

I am smiling.

Life is good.

No Jinx

I am almost to the tennis courts when I look ahead and see that Ashton is not alone. My heart sinks. I've blown it. I've missed my chance and now Ashton is walking with Nate and Rashan Tashman. I stop dead in my tracks. There is no way I am going to go up and talk to him with those guys around. I mean, they're nice and everything, but it just wouldn't be the same.

Dejected, I lean against the tall metal fence that goes around the tennis courts and watch Ashton, Nate, and Rashan disappear into three tiny specks. For a second I am really mad at myself for being late and missing my chance to walk with Ashton. But then I reach in my pocket, unfold the note, and read it again. And again.

I close my eyes and imagine the scene. Me and Ashton. A couple. Dancing *together*. Friday night . . .

Friday night? *Wait!* We have a game!

And so I spend the rest of the walk downtown thinking about how I will make sure Ashton knows I have a game without actually having to walk up and tell him myself (which we both know I could never do). I mean, I don't want him to think that I don't like him back or that I don't want to go to the dance, because I do. But I can't. From the bridge past the high school to the library, I send psychic messages to Logan Goldsmith to make Friday a team spirit day when we wear our jerseys to school. Then it would be so obvious. Ashton would know for sure.

When I finally walk into the library, the first thing I do is casually look around to see if I can spot Ashton. But he's nowhere in sight. I don't see Rashan or Nate either, but I do find Kiesha way in the back at the round table where we always sit. With all the excitement, the note, and the running, it's kind of hard to concentrate on math. But I have to snap out of it and pull myself together—we have a test on Friday. I push the note, Ashton, and the dance all into the back of my mind. Plus Kiesha's so nice, I don't want to be rude and not pay attention.

I really want to tell Kiesha about Ashton and the note and everything, but I have this weird feeling that I shouldn't even talk about it to anyone—not even Paige or Isabel. Because I've been thinking that everything is going so well, and I'm a little worried that if I actually talk about it, maybe it won't come true. And I know it sounds stupid because I did get the note and everything. But this feels so good. I don't want to jinx it. I think you know what I mean.

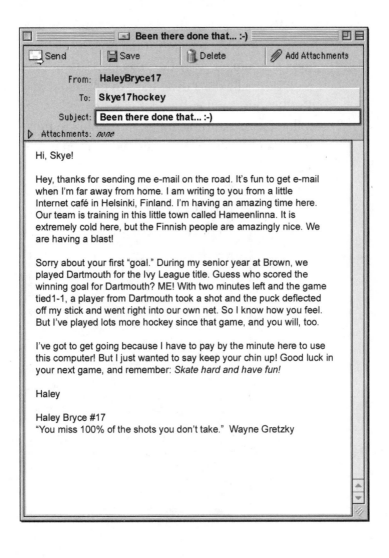

Been there done that... :-)

| Send | Save | Delete | Add Attachments |

From: **HaleyBryce17**

To: **Skye17hockey**

Subject: **Been there done that... :-)**

▷ Attachments: *none*

Hi, Skye!

Hey, thanks for sending me e-mail on the road. It's fun to get e-mail when I'm far away from home. I am writing to you from a little Internet café in Helsinki, Finland. I'm having an amazing time here. Our team is training in this little town called Hameenlinna. It is extremely cold here, but the Finnish people are amazingly nice. We are having a blast!

Sorry about your first "goal." During my senior year at Brown, we played Dartmouth for the Ivy League title. Guess who scored the winning goal for Dartmouth? ME! With two minutes left and the game tied 1-1, a player from Dartmouth took a shot and the puck deflected off my stick and went right into our own net. So I know how you feel. But I've played lots more hockey since that game, and you will, too.

I've got to get going because I have to pay by the minute here to use this computer! But I just wanted to say keep your chin up! Good luck in your next game, and remember: *Skate hard and have fun!*

Haley

Haley Bryce #17
"You miss 100% of the shots you don't take." Wayne Gretzky

Chicken Wings

We got beat *bad* this weekend. After our first game, everybody who ate at the pizza place got food poisoning. I ate at the pizza place. It was so bad, I actually don't even want to talk about it. But let's just say I spent a lot of time on the toilet, looking into the toilet, or running to the toilet, and I will never eat atomic chicken wings again—ever.

Ithaca 15U Comets fall to Rochester and Buffalo

The Ithaca 15U Comets dropped two games this weekend in Rochester. Saturday morning the Comets were held scoreless in a 5-0 loss to the Rochester Americans. Apple Jensen had 27 saves for Ithaca. In the second game of the day, the Comets came back to tie the Buffalo Bisons but ended up losing, 5-4, in overtime. Madison Gendelman, Cash Erickson, Sidney Johns, and Logan Goldsmith all had goals for the Comets. Nikki Wyatt, Jamie Hughes, and Abigail Dwyer each notched an assist. Rachel McKenna had 36 saves for the Comets. Ithaca returns to action Friday, December 3, in Watertown.

Pretty in Pink

It takes me three days to recover from puking my guts out. On Wednesday, Isabel comes over before school and brings me her pink T-shirt, and we both decide I should wear my new jeans. Isabel says I look "so cute"— these are her words, not mine. I actually think I do look pretty good, though, and even Shelby says something. She is half asleep on her way to the bathroom when she passes Isabel and me in the hall.

"Pink's your color, Skye," she says. Isabel and I look at each other and laugh. We both wonder if Shelby is actually walking in her sleep or something. But I think she really means it.

By ninth period I am anxiously awaiting my big walk downtown, but Mr. Thompson won't let us leave until all the chairs are up. This is ultra annoying. When he finally lets us go, I do a mad dash to my locker. I will not miss Ashton two Wednesdays in a row. When I turn the corner, I see Ashton standing with a whole bunch of boys at the end of the hallway.

Do not chicken out. Do not chicken out. Do not chicken out, I tell myself. I keep walking. I get closer, and Ashton looks right at me. He is waving and pointing outside, signaling that this is where we will meet. Paige watches the whole thing from her locker.

"Ooh-la-la!" she says, smiling and raising her eyebrows up and down. As usual my face turns all red and my heart starts pounding like a bass drum. And I am so distracted by how good everything is going and in such a rush to get outside that I slam my locker door and get half-way down the hall before I realize that I don't have my stupid math book. I run back, grab the book, and find Ashton outside by the buses.

Even though it's sunny and the sky is clear and bright, it's freezing outside. We both zip up our jackets and Ashton pulls out his red baseball cap—which looks very cute on him, by the way—and we head downtown. We mostly just talk about school, the Lakeview musical *Oliver!*, wrestling, and hockey. From the tennis courts to the first traffic light past the gas station, Ashton tells me how excited he is to finally get his cast off tomorrow. And how psyched he is to start wrestling again, even though he has to wait until after New Year's Day before he's allowed to actually practice.

Then, about a block before the library, right in front of the coffee shop, Ashton stops walking. He has this look on his face like he has something to tell me. My heart goes into overdrive. I have to concentrate hard not to smile.

This is it. This is the moment. I can't believe this is actually happening to *me*.

"Ahhh, did you forget something?" I ask nervously, hoping he will say, "Oh no, the only thing I forgot is to ask you out!" But that isn't it.

"No, just a sec—" he says, digging around for something in his backpack. "I thought you might like this." He hands me this wrinkled-up hockey card. "It's Cammi Granato, from the Olympic team," he says proudly.

Of course I know it's Cammi Granato, because I'm the one who's the hockey star here. But I pretend I'm surprised and examine it more closely. It is worn-out around the edges, like someone has been carrying it around in his wallet or something. I don't really care what kind of shape it's in. I mean, this is just the nicest, most thoughtful present ever.

My mind is gooey, and birds are flying around my head. I think I am in love. He is so nice! I am dying to tell someone. I am dying for Ashton to tell me he's the one—the note writer. I am dying for something to happen, something like you see in the movies.

But instead all I manage to squeeze out is "Thanks!"

Model Advice

I find Kiesha sitting by herself at the big round table in our usual spot in the back of the library. I am dying to tell her about Ashton. I am dying to show her the hockey card. I am bursting to tell her everything. She is cool and nice and older, and I know she'd tell me just what to do, just how to act.

"Hey," I say, smiling as I sit down next to her at the table.

"Hey right back at you," she replies. Kiesha has a big smile on her face, like she knows something. She leans toward me and whispers in my ear. "Skye," she teases, "who is that cute boy I always see you with?"

This is all the invitation I need. I tell her everything—and I mean everything. I tell her about the notebook incident, about the notes, about Nate whispering in my ear, about walking downtown, about seeing Ashton by my locker, about the locker crash incident. It all comes pouring out of me. And even though I have talked about this to Isabel and Paige, it's different with Kiesha. She's in college. And I'm positive she is going to give me the advice I've been looking for—like how can I get a guy to like me? And is there something special I can do to make Ashton like me more? So I ask her.

I can't believe these questions actually come out of my mouth, but they do. And I just have this feeling she will help me. I trust her. She is nice, and I don't think she'd ever embarrass me, or tell anyone, or do anything like that.

"Skye, I can tell you the most important advice in the world if you want to know it," Kiesha says, scooting her chair as close to mine as it can get and lowering her voice so the high-school kid at the next table can't hear us. "Boys are hard to figure out, aren't they?" she asks.

I roll my eyes and nod. I have this feeling she knows exactly how I feel.

"OK, well, the best advice I can give you—" Kiesha starts. She turns to me and looks me right in the eyes. "Well, it sounds a little simple and maybe even a little corny, but really it's true." I open my eyes wide and lean in, relieved someone is finally going to clue me in here. Kiesha puts her hand on my shoulder and gives it a squeeze just to emphasize her point. "Just be yourself," she says. "Any boy worth thinking about will dig you just the way you are."

Sure, easy for you to say, I think. I mean, Kiesha looks like one of those models you see in *Seventeen* magazine. She's perfect *and* smart *and* beautiful.

Somehow Kiesha can tell what I'm thinking. *"You* are beautiful! Just be yourself," she says. I smile at the compliment. And when she says it, I almost really believe her.

☐	▤ Bad break	▣▤

🖳 Send	💾 Save	🗑 Delete	📎 Add Attachments

From: **Skye17hockey**

To: **HaleyBryce17**

Subject: **Bad break**

▷ Attachments: *none*

Dear Haley,

Are you still in Finland? I'm doing pretty well. I've started this new thing I'm doing at practice. I am taking 50 shots before everyone gets out on the ice. I hope that will help! Guess what? My best friend, Apple (who is a goalie on my team), broke her wrist! Now she is out of hockey for almost the entire season and I won't get to see her hardly ever because we go to different schools. This Friday my team plays Watertown. They are supposed to be really good.

Sincerely,
Your biggest fan,
Yours truly,

Skye

Skye Beryl O'Shea #17

P.S. YOU ARE THE GREATEST!!!!!!
P.P.S. Write back soon!

Watertown

I'm sitting in homeroom on Friday with my blue Comets jersey on and my hair in pigtails (Team Spirit Day) when I hear it: Dr. Hernandez's morning announcement. "I'd like to wish good luck today to the following teams competing this weekend, which star some of our very own Lakeview students—boys' modified basketball, boys' modified wrestling, girls' modified basketball, girls' modified volleyball, and last but not least, the Ithaca Comets girls' hockey team. Good luck and go Lakeview!"

After the announcement I feel much less nervous about the note and the dance. Between seeing me in my jersey and hearing the morning announcements, I'm positive Ashton will know that I have a game and that I'm not missing the dance tonight on purpose. Everyone in homeroom, including Ms. Hahn, wishes me luck. "You'll have to tell us how you do, Skye. We want a full report Monday," she says. She is so nice.

Later, I'm sitting on a purple and gold bench in the cramped Watertown locker room. I retie my skates five times, which is a lot even for me. I am nervous. I don't want to mess up. My superstitions are kicking in. I keep lacing my skates, then unlacing and retightening them until they feel just right. And I always lace up my left skate first and then my right, never the other way around. That would be complete bad luck. And yes, in case you are wondering, I am definitely a little worried that someone is going to notice me doing these weird superstitions.

Logan is sitting right next to me. "Little O, are those skates tight enough yet?" she asks.

"Ahhhh . . ." I stammer, searching for something to say. "New laces." I lie—I have to. There is no way anyone could understand my rituals. They're too hard to explain. Plus, I'm sure everyone would think I'm really weird.

Right before we leave the locker room, Coach Cosgrove and Lauren come in to give us our pep talk. "Girls," says Coach Cosgrove, "we don't practice every week so we can just go out there and lollygag around. I want to see some hustle and hard work out there tonight. Now go out and have some fun!" he says, pumping his fist in the air.

"Yeah!" we shout back, and jump up to line up behind Rachel. I am in line behind Jamie Hughes.

"Wait, girls. One more thing," Coach Cosgrove shouts above the chatter. "I had to do some shuffling today with Madison sick. Skye, you are right wing with Logan and Sidney today."

There is complete silence. Jamie turns

around, her eyes wide open, her jaw dropped. "You go, girl!" she whispers, patting me on the shoulder pads. Everyone looks pretty surprised, and I suddenly get the feeling that nobody is used to a sixth grader on the first line.

Lauren smiles at me. "You can do it, Skye! Now is the time to shine!" she says. I follow the line out the door and walk down the long hallway to the rink. My heart is beating a mile a minute, but for some reason I am more excited than nervous.

When we get out on the ice, loud warm-up music is booming from the giant speakers next to the scoreboard. Everyone is pumped. It's fun to play at night—there is even a crowd in the stands. Parents are cheering, music is blaring, and because they're so nice, Logan and Sidney stretch out next to me by the blue line.

"OK, Skye, we're going to kick some butt out there!" Sidney says, smiling. Then we all do this head-butt thing with our helmets.

Logan pats me on the back. "It's all you, O'Shea!" she says. I skate over to the huddle. My head is growing bigger by the second. I can't believe I'm on the *first line!*

Right off the bat, on the third shift out, I make a sweet pass to Logan as we cross the blue line into Watertown's zone. Logan takes the puck to the net and scores! Logan and Sidney practically knock me to the ice in celebration. We win 4-1. And it isn't like Watertown is bad or anything, because actually, they are pretty good. But our team is unstoppable. It is magic.

ASSIST!

| Send | Save | Delete | Add Attachments |

From: **Skye17hockey**
To: **HaleyBryce17**
Subject: **ASSIST!**
Attachments: *none*

Dear Haley,

I know you're probably really busy but I just wanted to tell you one great thing! We won today against Watertown 4-1 and I got an assist AND I played on the first line! That's all I wanted to tell you! How are you? I hope you're great.

Your biggest fan,
Yours truly,

Skye #17

YOUTH SPORTS ROUNDUP — TOMPKINS COUNTY

Youth Hockey

Comets Ice Watertown

Logan Goldsmith notched a season-high three goals and one assist as the Ithaca 15U Comets defeated Watertown 4-1 Friday at the Watertown Ice Arena. Rachel McKenna stopped 21 shots for the Comets. Anna Sylvester of Lansing added a goal and an assist for the victors. Skye O'Shea, Cash Erickson and Jenna Robbins all had assists for Ithaca. The Comets' next contest is on Sunday at Camilus.

Ithaca Travel defeat Lysander

Cole Olson and Bryant Montgomery each skated away with two goals as the Ithaca Squirt Travel team beat Lysander 4-3 in Lysander. Aubrey Ford and Kevin Flynn both had two assists in the overtime win. Caleb Church stopped 27 shots for the red. Next weekend the Ithaca Squirts will compete in the prestigious Silver Stick Tournament in Rome, N.Y.

GRADUATES: COR UNIVERSITY

Jonathan Peck, Ithac
Mecha

Celebrity Status

By Wednesday, the news is out. Ms. Hahn cuts the hockey article out of the paper and posts it on the "In the News" board by the pencil sharpener. "Way to go, Skye!" she says.

And in study hall, when Mr. Dean says something about my assist in front of the entire class, I'm feeling like the queen of Lakeview. "We have two celebrities among us today," he says, and then he reads both the Comets article and the one about Cole's team that was right next to it in the paper. Cole is in my study hall, too. I smile. Cole smiles. Everyone in study hall looks at us and smiles. By lunchtime I am feeling like a major big deal.

Besides my brush with fame, this morning Isabel lent me her blue overalls and orange T-shirt and I am feeling ultra stylish. Top this all off with the fact that on this very same day, I get my first "check plus" from Mrs. Mitchell. "Great!" is written across the top. I can't wait to show Kiesha.

When ninth period is over and the bell rings, I rush down to my locker eager to meet up with Ashton. But Ashton isn't waiting by my locker, or in the hallway, or in front by the buses (I look).

The entire way downtown, I cross my fingers and hope Ashton will come running up behind me. I keep turning around to look for him, but nobody is there.

I am almost to the tennis courts when I hear someone calling my name. "Skye! Skye! *Wait up!*"

Yes. Thank you. Ashton—he's coming. I turn around to wait for him. But as he gets closer, my big smile melts. It isn't Ashton. It's Nate. My heart sinks until I come up with the great idea that maybe—just maybe—Nate is coming to deliver a special message from Ashton. Like how Ashton is sorry he can't walk with me, or how he really missed me at the dance. Or maybe Nate's going to deliver another note to me. I smile with relief and wait for him to catch up.

"Hey, Skye!" Nate says, nervously smiling.

"Hey," I say back. "OK, let's cut the chitchat. Where's Ashton?" (OK, you're right. I do not say this. You know I would never say this. But seriously, I am definitely thinking this in a major way.)

"Hey, can I walk with you?" Nate asks.

"Sure," I shrug.

"Cool," he says.

That's it? Cool? *Isn't there anything else you want to say?* I think. To tell you the truth, it is awkward. Nate and I walk the entire way to the library and neither of us says one word. By the coffee shop I finally break the silence and ask him why he isn't at wrestling. He tells me there is a meet today, and only the varsity is going. I am dying to ask him where Ashton is, but I chicken out. I am hoping he brings this up soon.

We walk together the whole way to the library, but it isn't at all like walking with Ashton. Other than telling me why he doesn't have wrestling, Nate doesn't say a single word! When we walk up the stairs to the library, Nate stops and grabs my arm. I feel kind of weird, because there is something about Nate that gives me the creeps.

"Ahhh . . ." he says. He is staring at me, still holding my arm. I shake my arm away. "Can we do this again next week?" he asks nervously.

I am frozen. I don't know what to say. I am hoping Kiesha will walk up and save me. I am wishing I could just snap my fingers and disappear like Sabrina the Teenage Witch.

I shrug my shoulders. "Ahhh, I guess so" is all I can muster.

"Cool," he replies.

All I can say back is "Sure." I walk to the back of the library to meet Kiesha. *I am so stupid! Why did I say "Sure"?* I mean, not to be rude, but I do not want to walk with Nate. We have absolutely nothing in common. Plus, whenever he's around me, he just stares at me and doesn't say anything.

To make matters worse, when I get to the table in the back of the library, Kiesha is not waiting for me as she usually is. I sit and wait. I am weirded out by the whole Nate thing and I also am beginning to get a little worried about Kiesha. She's never late. I scrounge thirty-five cents from the very bottom of my backpack and call my mom from the pay phone by the bathrooms. The hospital receptionist pages her, and she picks up the phone in the delivery room. I can tell she's not happy that I have called her at work.

"Skye, this had better be an emergency because I really can't talk!" I explain the situation and beg her to come pick me up. "Honey," she says, suddenly using this sugary sweet voice that she only uses when there are other people around, "first of all, I'm standing in the delivery room about ten minutes away from delivering a baby. You know I can't pick you up, sweetheart. Kiesha is probably just running late."

"But Mommmmmmm," I say, whining.

"Why don't you try doing your homework or reading a book?" she says. "Skye, you can't possibly be bored in a library!"

"Mom, please, *pleeeease* come pick me up!" I have resorted to begging.

"I'm sorry, sweetheart. I really have to run—"

And the next thing I hear is a dial tone.

I return to my stuff and put my head down on the table and wait. I have two more hours until my dad will be here to get me. I can't really do my homework because, first of all, I don't really get any of it, especially math. Second of all, I can't stop thinking about Ashton and Nate and all this stupid, idiotic boy stuff—which I wish I could just stop thinking about, but I can't.

Seven Minutes

When I finally get home, I wolf down a peanut-butter-and-jelly sandwich and wait for my mom by the back door. She's supposed to pick me up and take me to practice, but she's late. When she finally drops me off, I run all the way from the parking lot, through the lobby, to the locker room. Hockey bags are scattered across the floor. Everyone else is already out on the ice. I slip on my skates and tie them faster than I think I ever have in my entire life. But it doesn't matter how much I rush. I'm late. Way late.

Seven minutes late.

As I step out onto the ice, something Coach Cosgrove said is rattling in my head— something about being on time, dedication, and commitment. It's not looking good. Coach is talking to the team at center ice, but he stops in mid-sentence when I skate up. Everybody looks at me. I am ultra embarrassed, and my face turns red.

"Oh, hello, Skye. Nice of you to join us today," Coach says, joking. But then he gets kind of serious. "Seventy," he says, hitting the ice with his stick to signal I should get down on my belly and start doing push-ups. "You can give me ten push-ups for every minute you were late."

Seventy push-ups! Do you know how hard

this is? My arms begin to shake and quiver at twenty. After thirty he lets me kneel and do half push-ups. When I finish, my arms feel like wet noodles, and I swear to myself I will never be late again.

At home I brush my teeth and splash warm water on my face, trying to forget about my miserable day.

"Skye," my mom yells from the bottom of the stairs.

"What?" I manage to answer, even though I have a mouthful of toothpaste.

"Kiesha left a message on my voice mail today—"

"Yeah? And?" I shout downstairs.

"And she has the flu. She tried to call the school before you left, but I guess the office couldn't catch you in time. She felt really bad about it."

So, as it turns out, my walk downtown was for nothing. I mean, I'm not mad at Kiesha because really it wasn't her fault. But this week isn't turning out so great, and I hope it gets better soon.

It Doesn't Get Any Better

The very next day I am in seventh-period study hall when Mr. Dean asks for a volunteer. "Who wants to run this note down to the main office and this book to the library?" he asks, holding up a book and a pink referral notice (which is folded in half so you can't read it and see who's in trouble). As luck would have it, my hand is the first one Mr. Dean sees. "Ms. O'Shea," he says, motioning me to the front of the room and handing the book and the note to me. "Thank you for your good citizenship."

It's not like I have anything better to do. I'm done with all my homework, even math. And Paige is at her orthodontist appointment, so we can't pass notes back and forth like we usually do.

First I go to the library and drop off the book. When I get to the main office, Dr. Hernandez's secretary is on the phone. I hand her the note. "Thanks," she mouths, her hand cupped over the phone. Since I have fifteen whole minutes left until the period is over, I get the bright idea to take the long way back. Anything is better than being bored to tears in study hall.

I am feeling mischievous as I walk down the empty halls and peer into busy classrooms. At first I feel like I'm going to get caught, but the longer I wander, the more fun it gets. I stop in front of Mr. Jordan's health room and check out all the posters on his bulletin board. I wander by Ms. French's room. The door is open and I sneak a wave at Isabel. This is kind of fun. I head toward the band room to see if I can spot Olivia and Grace in orchestra.

As I round the corner by the band room, I hear a sound coming from behind the auditorium doors. It's a girl and a boy giggling. I don't know who they are, and I'm kind of embarrassed hearing them. I mean, they obviously don't know I'm listening.

"Shhh . . ." whispers the boy.

"OK, OK . . . do you think we'll get in trouble?" the girl asks.

My ears get tingly. I don't exactly hurry away. OK, I don't even move, because in some weird way I am enjoying this—it's kind of funny. I stand there in the hallway eavesdropping, trying to picture who could be behind the doors. Finally I decide I'd better keep walking toward the band room before whoever is back there sees me. I start walking away but stop when I hear footsteps.

I turn and look back. I can barely make out the silhouettes of a boy and girl standing in front of the big bulletin board at the end of the hallway. They do not see me because they are too busy kissing—and I mean the noisy, saliva kind of kissing.

I stand motionless at the end of the hallway and stare back at them. I can't see the boy's face, but I recognize the girl. It's Brooke Benton, my "friend" from the locker room leg-hair incident. When I see that it's her, I feel weird watching, but I also kind of want to keep watching. I stand there for a few more seconds—they are so pre-occupied, they don't even notice me. I turn to walk away. I take a few steps, but I can't resist looking one more time. I turn and—

And—

Oh my gosh.

I am hoping very hard that I have not just seen what I think I saw. I am hoping very hard that if I look one more time, it won't be him. It will just be someone who looks like him. My heart is expanding in my chest. I quickly dart into the empty entranceway to the band room so that the kissers can't see me.

Maybe I'm wrong. Maybe that was some other guy. Finally, I take one more peek, poking my head around the corner. His back is toward me so he does not see me, but I see him. It is him—I'm sure. It's Ashton.

My heart does this sinking, panging, hurting thing that I've never felt before this very moment. My head is sweaty and hot. I am dizzy like I just stepped off a roller coaster. I lean back against the wall and shut my eyes.

This is not a good feeling.

I do not like this feeling.

My stomach is churning.

I want to get out of here. I want to press Erase, or Un-do, or Rewind. I want a do-over. I want to go back in time and not volunteer to take the stupid book back for Mr. Dean in the first place.

But all I can do is wait there in the entrance-way until I'm sure Ashton and Brooke are gone. After what seems like forever, I scrape myself up and manage to make it back to study hall.

"Nice to see you again, Skye," Mr. Dean says when I walk back into the room. I try to act as cool as I can, like nothing unusual happened—like I just took a detour to the bathroom or something. "Did you misunderstand me and think I wanted you to return the book to a library in China?" Mr. Dean asks, laughing and looking at his watch. He thinks he is very funny. I fake a smile as best I can, slump back down in my seat, and stare at the clock until the bell finally rings.

And I would like to ask you just one question. What was I ever thinking that would give me the crazy idea that Ashton liked me?

I feel like an idiot.

Ripped Up

It has been one week since I saw what I saw. I pile up my stupid secret-admirer notes and rip them into tiny little pieces. I don't even know if Ashton wrote them, but I'm through liking him. At least, this is what I tell myself—even though every time I see him, my heart still beats fast and butterflies invade my stomach.

The truth is, no matter how hard I try, I can't seem to stop liking Ashton. It's not like I have a switch I can just turn off or something. And when he sees me, he doesn't act different or weird or anything. He acts the same way he used to. He's as nice and sweet and cute as before. Paige even still thinks he likes me (that's assuming he ever *did* like me in the first place). But if he likes me, then he has a funny way of showing it. Ashton and Brooke are now an official couple. Paige saw them holding hands in the back of the band room, and Grace says she always sees them passing notes in social studies. So I have tried to accept this fact and get him out of my mind—only I can't.

And if you know how I can, please tell me fast.

Three Days Later

As if it wasn't enough that my love life is in shambles, my family life seems to be going down the drain, too. Like today, I don't know how it all started, but we are sitting at the kitchen table when my dad erupts like a volcano. He shoves his plate toward the center of the table, gets up out of his seat, and storms out the back door, slamming the door so hard behind him that the entire house shakes and the framed photo on the wall crashes to the floor. There is glass everywhere.

This is about the time I start to cry. I hate it when my parents fight. OK, I'm not just crying, I'm sobbing. Tears are rolling down my cheeks and dropping like a waterfall into my spaghetti. That's when Shannon starts everything.

"Skye, you are such a little baby. Would you just *shut up*?" she says, turning to me and sneering. And this is when I kind of lose it. OK, I don't "kind of" lose it, I *definitely* lose it. I reach over my plate and shove her—hard.

Shannon lunges at me, shoving me back even harder. My glass of orange juice crashes to the floor. My sister is now strangling me to death right there at the kitchen table.

"Girls!" my mom yells. But it doesn't help. My sister has me in a professional-wrestling headlock. "Girls, stop it this instant!" Mom shouts louder. But Shannon won't let go.

And it hurts. And there is nothing I can do, except . . . except, well—

I bite her.

I know it sounds gross and disgusting, but it works. The moment I sink my two front teeth into her arm Shannon lets go of me. My mom is not happy. She is screaming. "All three of you go to your rooms this instant!" she shouts.

"What? I didn't do anything!" Shelby yells. And actually, she is kind of innocent. But since when do I stick up for her?

It doesn't matter. My mom doesn't seem to care who did what. "You are all punished!" she screams, then turns and points her finger at me. "You, young lady, can forget about any sleepovers for the next month, and I will think about whether you will be going to your hockey tournament."

"WHAT?" I scream. No way! *No way!* There is no way she can take away hockey.

Next she lays into my sisters. "I cannot tell you how furious I am at both of you," she says, looking mostly at Shannon. "May I remind you that you are older than Skye? You should know better than to egg her on like that!" Then she drops the bomb. "You can both count yourselves out of the winter formal, because you are not going—period."

"WHAT?" they shout in unison as they leave the table, maneuvering through the river of spilled orange juice and broken glass and starting up the stairs.

"You can go, too," my mom says, looking at me with disgust and pointing upstairs. When I get to my room I slam my door behind me.

"Skye," Shannon shouts through the wall, "you are such an annoying little brat!"

"I hate everyone in this stupid family!" Shelby cries over and over again.

I collapse on my bed with my pillow over my head, my nose smushed up against the mattress. There is no way on earth my mom can do this to me. She can say no sleepovers, no TV, no computer, or anything else she wants, but she can't take away *hockey*. Really, it's the only thing I have.

Trouble

My mom is sitting on the edge of my bed. She looks tired. Her eyes are red. I am feeling very guilty, as if I've made everything worse for her. "Are you and Dad getting divorced?" I blurt out, tears trickling down my cheeks. Her whole face changes, like she isn't mad at me anymore.

"Of course not!" she says, looking as if this is the strangest question she has ever heard. Then she gives me this big talk about how sometimes people just disagree on things, even when they love each other very much. She says that I have to realize that's just how my dad is— he has a bad temper. He has a lot of pressures at work right now, and I have to not get upset every time he gets mad. She says he's not mad at us, he's just stressed out about work. Then she gives me this big lecture about how I need to not fight so much with my sisters and how biting is "absolutely unacceptable in this household." By the time my mom is finally done lecturing me, I notice that she doesn't seem that mad anymore.

Does this mean I won't really be punished? Maybe she has realized that this entire fiasco wasn't my fault! Right then and there, it's as if my mom reads my mind. "Skye, I'm glad we had this talk," she says. "But I hope you understand, you are still one-hundred-percent punished.

What you did was utterly unacceptable. Your father and I will not tolerate that kind of behavior."

"But Shannon—" I try to defend myself.

"I don't care what your sister did to you. You bit her, and that's disgusting, Skye—really. And I don't want to see that type of behavior ever again." She begins to get up and walk toward the door. There's no hug, no "I love you," no nothing.

I am really depressed. I am picturing having to call Coach Cosgrove and tell him I can't play. But my mom stops just before the door and looks at me.

"For the next two weeks you are punished— no TV, no sleepovers, no friends over, no movies, no computer, and no going to the mall. The only thing your father and I will permit you to do is—"

I am praying.

I am crossing my fingers.

Please, please, please.

"—is hockey," she says. "And that's only because you have made a commitment to your team, and you know how we feel about commitments."

Air slowly comes into my lungs. Trumpets are sounding. I am free!

Happy Holidays

I have one more day of school (and an entire week in purgatory to spend with my family) before I go to Lake Placid next weekend with my team. This morning at breakfast, my mom tells me I have fifteen minutes to make a thank-you card for Kiesha. It is supposed to be a "thank-you" and "happy holidays" card all wrapped into one. I draw a Santa Claus with a volleyball and draw a menorah, too, just in case she's Jewish. I'm half Jewish and half Unitarian, so I'm sensitive to these things. My mom takes the card without even telling me if she likes it or not and puts it in an envelope with a check. "All college students like money!" she says, licking the envelope shut and handing it back to me.

I make it through the last day of school. I get three projects back and actually do well on all of them. Ms. Hahn especially likes my time capsule entry. "This is fabulous, Skye!" she says, smiling as she hands it back to me. She is such a good teacher.

Time Capsule Contest

In celebration of the new millennium, Lakeview Middle School is happy to participate in the City of Ithaca's time capsule project. The time capsule will be buried this spring at Stewart Park and will remain buried there until December 31, 2009. There will be a bronze marker with directions for future citizens of Ithaca to open our capsule in one hundred years! This project is sponsored by *The Ithaca Tribune*. Using this form, please write a letter to future Ithacans. In your letter, make sure to include what object you are burying with your letter, and why. Please keep it to 500 words or less.

Hello,

My name is Skye Beryl O'Shea. I will tell you right now where the Beryl comes from because everybody always asks. I'm named after this famous explorer pilot named Beryl Markham and even though it's kind of an unusual name, I think it's kind of cool. I am in the sixth grade at Lakeview Middle School in Ithaca, NY. I live in a neighborhood right next to Cornell University.

Hockey is my favorite thing to do. Hockey is a big thing in Ithaca. You might not play hockey, maybe you play a game floating in space, and maybe you don't even drive cars, just spaceships. Since hockey might not even exist anymore, I am including a hockey puck with this letter. It is made of rubber and it's hard.

I hope by the time you read this, I will be a famous hockey star and maybe they will change the name of Lakeview to Skye Beryl O'Shea Middle School. You never know!

I hope you are enjoying life in Ithaca and that there is peace in the world. I hope that schools don't give homework anymore and you'll just get to go to school and do fun things and go on field trips everyday. I hope the cures for cancer and AIDS have been invented, and that there is no more racism or sexism. I hope there have been many women presidents by the time you read this. Maybe one will have been me.

Happy New Year!

Yours Very Truly,

Skye #17

skye Beryl O'Shea

I am not trying to be rude, but all day long I am really, really hoping that I do not have to walk downtown with Nate after school. I am hoping he has forgotten, that he has wrestling with Ashton, or that he has left town for winter vacation. And for once I get my wish. Nate is not at my locker, and I don't exactly stick around and wait to see if he shows up.

It snows the entire way to the library, but I don't care. The snow's pretty, and it's winter break! I get there early and check my e-mail since I've lost computer privileges at home. I have one e-mail from Haley. And after Kiesha and I go over all my math homework, I pull out the card and the math test I got back today—I got an 87! Kiesha says this is the best present I could ever give her.

| 🔲 Send | 💾 Save | 🗑 Delete | 📎 Add Attachments |

From: **HaleyBryce17**

To: **Skye17hockey**

Subject: **Sweden**

▷ Attachments: *none*

Hej! Skye (That's hello in Swedish!),

I'm writing you from my host family's, the Olofssons', computer in
Stockholm. Stockholm is the capital city of Sweden. We are here
for two weeks of training and will be playing the Swedish National
Team at the end of our stay. Stockholm is a beautiful city—chilly,
but beautiful. The Olofssons have three kids and they all play hockey!
Lars is 11, Erika is 14, and Hanna is 16. Awesome news on the assist!
Remember, with no assists, there would be no goals! You go, girl!
Keep working hard on and off the ice. You can do it!
God natt! (good night),

Haley

Haley Bryce #17

"Shoot for the moon; if you miss you'll land among the stars."
Les Brown

P.S. I'm going to throw an autographed picture from our goalie,
Beatrice McKay, in the mail, and you can give it to Apple to cheer
her up.

Happy New Year

Just in case you have never done it, let me be the first to tell you—it is very depressing to spend New Year's Eve by yourself. My mom and dad are at the New Year's Eve Ball at the hospital and my sisters are at a hockey tournament in Toronto. This leaves me home alone, completely by myself. Apple and Summer went to New York City. They invited me, but of course my idiotic parents wouldn't let me go. Apparently I am still grounded.

"Skye," my mom told me, "until you show us you can make mature decisions and act responsibly, you are not going to have the privileges you enjoy. That means you can't go around biting people when you get angry with them." She cannot seem to forget this little incident and has managed to remind me of it every single day of vacation, even on New Year's Eve. "There's pizza in the freezer, and my cell phone number's on the counter," she says, quickly kissing me on the forehead and rushing out the door. I hear the garage door opening and watch through the kitchen window as my dad's truck disappears into the snowy night.

I open the fridge and look around for something to eat, but I'm not hungry. I hate frozen pizza. I am bored! Soooo bored.

Seriously, there is nothing to do in this house. I walk toward my room, but somehow I end up in my sisters' room. I'm supposedly not allowed in here. My sisters would kill me if they found out, which is exactly why it's fun to be in here. I creep around the room, and even though my sisters are in Toronto, I'm still worried they can see me—as if they have a little video camera standing guard for them, recording every move I make. I almost leave, but I'm still really mad at them. I mean, if it wasn't for them, I'd be in New York City right now with Summer and Apple. Plus, I remind myself, there is not a soul in this house except me. Nobody will ever know.

I sit down at Shannon's desk, open the top drawer, and start sifting around. Shannon keeps everything immaculately neat and organized. The top of her desk is like a museum. Everything is labeled. The cup with pens in it says "PENS" in neat black block lettering. Even the blank paper piled up in a tray is labeled "PAPER," as if she would forget what it is. I begin to think Shannon may have set a trap for me—you know, to catch me. So I move over to Shelby's desk. Shelby's stuff is organized, too, but not like Shannon's. Shelby is easier to be snoopy with. There's more stuff kind of lying around. I poke through all her drawers and folders until I finally find something good.

Shel,

What's up, girl? I am writing you from study hall because I have done virtually every single assignment I can think of, including physics — impressive, don't ya think? How is hockey? I am going to come to your next home game. When is it? Have you and Shannon decided where you are going next year? I've applied early decision to Princeton. That's my first choice. But we'll see. By the way, a certain boy you are in love with happens to be sitting two rows away from me this very second. I can see he's writing your name with little hearts all over the front of his American history notebook... psych! ☺ Speaking of Ramsey, have I told you how bummed I am that you and Shannon can't go to winter formal? Completely unfair! It really stinks. Especially since I'm almost positive Ramsey was going to ask you. Zach told me, and I'm pretty sure he's right. Siblings are totally annoying. I sympathize completely. Tyler is the biggest brat in the world — worse than Skye. Well, GTG, the bell's about to ring ☹ Call me tonight!
Luv ya lots,
Abby

Well, Abby obviously heard only one side of the story, I think to myself, rolling my eyes. I carefully fold the note along the worn creases and sift back through the folders on the top of Shelby's desk. The house is so quiet that it's freaking me out. I look around again to see if anyone is watching, and then I stick the note in the same spot I found it. Shelby will never know.

I leave my sisters' room exactly as I found it and go into my mom's study. I am bored. I can't even instant message anybody—it's part of my punishment. "If you don't know how to communicate civilly with your sisters, you will not be afforded the luxury of communicating with your friends," my mom said, just before she unplugged the keypad and mouse and locked them in her file drawer. So I haven't been able to write Haley, check my e-mail, or anything, and now it's quiet, dark, and spooky in this house and I don't like one bit being left home completely by myself. There are weird noises. My dad always says it's just the house settling, but I keep thinking there is somebody peering in the front window in the family room. I lock myself in my room and push my dresser against my door, just in case.

To tell you the truth, my vacation has been extremely, entirely, absolutely, positively *boring*! And I can't believe I'm saying this, but I'm actually kind of excited for school to start. That will be our little secret.

Ugh

Did I say I wanted to go back to school? Scratch that. I've been back only three days and I already have eight billion tons of homework. Kiesha went to California with her volleyball team, so I don't see her till next week. I saw Ashton twice today with Brooke. And the worst thing is that when he looks at me, he still smiles. So maybe he *was* my secret admirer. I am getting a pimple on my chin. I don't really have much else to say.

Happy New Year!			
Send	Save	Delete	Add Attachments

From: **Skye17hockey**

To: **HaleyBryce17**

Subject: **Happy New Year!**

Attachments: *none*

Haley,

Are you still in Sweden? I am in Ithaca. Happy New Year! What did you do for New Year's? I did nothing, except I did stay up until one in the morning. Our next tournament is in Lake Placid. We are going to play in the Olympic rink! I wish your team was there, but I know you're not. It will still be cool, though. Well, I just wanted to say hi. So hi!

Yours very truly,

Skye

Skye O'Shea #17
P.S. Apple says thanks for the picture!

Lake Placid

I lug my hockey bag, my jerseys, my pillow, and my green overnight duffle bag downstairs, through the garage, and into my mom's van. My mom's dropping all my stuff off at the Sylvesters' on her way to work tomorrow, so when they pick me up at Lakeview after fourth period, we'll head straight for our hockey tournament in Lake Placid.

My mom even packed me a gourmet lunch for the five-hour ride. I look in the fridge to check it out myself:

Two peanut-butter-and-jelly sandwiches
Two bags of salt-and-vinegar potato chips
(my favorite)
Three sodas (even though they are the
gross natural kind)
A plateful of brownies for dessert

"Share them with the Sylvesters, honey," my mom reminds me as I close the fridge.

I know my mom feels bad she can't go. Of course she has to work at the hospital. "Skye, honey," she tells me on my way up to bed, "my patients count on me. I'm sorry."

Whatever. My sisters have a tournament in New Jersey so my dad's going with them. But I don't really care who is going, because I am so excited and you will see why—

	Lake Placid...	
Send	Save	Delete	Add Attachments

From: **HaleyBryce17**

To: **Skye17hockey**

Subject: **Lake Placid...**

▷ Attachments: *none*

Hey, Skye!

I'm back at home in Minnesota. We're home for a week and then we fly to Calgary for a game against Team Canada! It feels great to be home. Now I have a ton of laundry to do, letters to read, and bills to pay. I'll get to spend time with my boyfriend, Liam, and my dogs, Gretzky and Mario. I'm also applying to medical school, so I have a ton of work to do!

Good luck with your tourney in Lake Placid! I wish I were going to be at the Olympic Training Center while you were there. But I have set up a little surprise for you. When you get there, have your coach call Keri Nash at the OTC (324-1300). She has a little surprise in store for you. Let me know how it goes! Good luck in your tournament!
Haley ;-)

Haley Bryce #17
"If you think you can or you think you can't, you're right!"
Henry Ford

It's in the Past

We pull up to the Olympic Inn around 4:30 and find most of our team already gathered in the main lodge, sprawled out on three couches around a big stone fireplace. Everybody is excited about the indoor swimming pool, the hot tub, and the fact that Mrs. Goldsmith, Logan's mom, tells us the players are all sharing rooms (instead of staying with parents as we normally do). I get a room with Anna, Tessa, and Sidney, which is just fine by me. The only person I really don't want to room with is Abigail Dwyer. Anna, Tessa, Sidney, and I all bring our stuff up to our room on the third floor. We call who gets what bed and then run back down to the team meeting in the lobby.

As soon as I walk in, I spot Coach Cosgrove talking to Madison's mom by the front desk. I walk over and wait until they're done. Finally Mrs. Gendelman walks away, and I reach deep into my jeans pocket and pull out Haley's e-mail note. I hand it to Coach Cosgrove.

"This looks interesting," he says, unfolding it carefully. I watch as Coach Cosgrove's eyes open wide. His eyebrows rise high as he reads the letter. "Wow, Skye! That's terrific! I didn't realize you were friends with Olympic champions!" he says loudly, announcing it to the entire lobby.

Soon everyone wants to see, and my e-mail from Haley gets passed around the crowd of parents and players in the lobby. I am a big hit. Coach Cosgrove doesn't waste any time. He pulls out his cell phone and dials the number in Haley's note. As everyone realizes what he's doing, the room falls silent. Our entire team and all the parents wait to hear what our surprise is. "Well," Coach Cosgrove says, closing his phone and pausing, as if he has bad news. Then he smiles broadly, building up the suspense. "We are scheduled for a personal tour of the locker room used by the U.S. Women's Olympic Hockey Team!" The lobby erupts in cheers as everybody next to me pats me on the back.

"Awesome!" Sidney shouts.

"You rule, Skye!" echoes Cash.

"Yeah, O'Shea!" says Madison, practically tackling me with a hug.

Later that night we have our first game against the Kitchener Falcons. The rink is right across the street from our hotel. Our entire team meets in the lobby, and at 6:45 sharp we hoist our heavy hockey bags over our shoulders and hike across the snowy street to the arena. The Olympic rink is ultra deluxe. It's the biggest rink I've ever seen. Plus I keep thinking about how this is where Haley practices. Maybe it will bring me luck.

It brings no luck at all. We get annihilated by the Falcons, 9-2. It is depressing. We all play really badly. I mean *really* badly, and we know it. After the game, Lauren and Coach Cosgrove enter the locker room. We are all hanging our heads. Nobody seems to be able to even look Coach Cosgrove or Lauren in the eye. The room is silent.

And then, without saying anything, Coach Cosgrove tears off the back cover of the tournament program and tapes the blank side up on the wall with a piece of hockey tape. He takes out a thick black marker and writes "Kitchener 9, Comets 2."

Then, silently, Lauren walks over, tears the paper off the wall, and rips it into little tiny pieces. Apparently they are working together on this, but I can tell by the looks on the other players' faces that nobody really gets what is going on. When Lauren is done ripping up the paper, she walks around the quiet locker room and hands each of us a little piece of Coach Cosgrove's sign. We all look at the paper, puzzled, not having any clue what we are supposed to do with it.

"As far as I'm concerned, that game is completely over. It's in the past," Coach Cosgrove says, crumpling up his piece of the sign and tossing it into the trash can sitting in the center of the locker room.

Lauren crumples up hers, too, and tosses it into the trash. "It's in the past," she says, just like Coach Cosgrove.

One by one, we all crumple up our pieces of the sign and pitch them in the garbage. "It's in the past," says Logan, cracking a smile and turning to Jamie.

"It's in the past," says Jamie, almost laughing.

"It's in the past," I say, grinning, feeling a little stupid. But that's what everyone else is saying, so I say it, too. And one by one, everyone follows suit.

Magically, everyone starts looking better. Logan is smiling now, and so is Cash. Lauren and Coach Cosgrove walk toward the door. Coach Cosgrove turns around just as he is leaving.

"I trust you will come here to play tomorrow, and play the way I know you are capable of playing," he says. Then he leaves the room, the door swinging behind him.

Surprise

I am in the locker room, carefully taping my new stick. I use Shannon's technique, spinning the blue tape around the top end of my stick until I have just a little notch, one that's not too big. Next I move down to the blade, slowly wrapping black tape around and around until the entire blade is covered. I pat the tape down, making sure there are no wrinkles. I am sure this stick is lucky—I just have a feeling about it. I finish it off by sprinkling a little bit of baby powder on the sticky black tape on the blade, closing my eyes, and lightly kissing the sweet spot where the puck goes. I know this sounds weird, but it's just something I've always done, and I'm not about to change it now.

We have seventeen minutes until we play in the championship game of the tournament. After our terrible showing against the Kitchener Falcons, we beat Salmon River and the Wisconsin Challengers to move into the championship game against the Halton Hills Twisters.

Everybody is nervous. We each take a while to warm up, shake off our nerves, and settle down. But by the third period we are tied, 2-2. I'm playing really well, which I am attributing to my new stick and the fact that this is Haley's home rink. I just feel lucky today. So it's no surprise, really, when I find myself wide open in the slot on our second power play of the game.

"Jamie!" I scream, raising my stick above my head so that she'll spot me. I'm open—wide open.

I wave my stick again, this time not yelling out. By some stroke of luck, Jamie spots me. She slides a perfect pass from the blue line directly to me in front of the goalie. Suddenly everything goes into slow motion. I put all my weight behind my shot and watch in wonder as the puck sails effortlessly off my new stick, past the goalie's outstretched glove, and into the upper left-hand corner of the net.

It's in.

It's in!

I scored!

Jamie practically knocks me down with a hug in front of the net. "Yeah, O'Shea!" she shouts.

"Go, girl!" screams Tessa, pounding me on my helmet.

"It's all you, Skye!" says Logan before she jumps on the rest of us, knocking us all to the ice.

I skate to the bench, where my teammates are all standing, hands outstretched to congratulate me. I go down the line and give everyone a high five before I hop over the boards by the far door and collapse onto the bench. I am breathing heavily and look down at the floor until I catch my breath. Then I look up at the stands, and that's when I see him.

My dad.

I have to look twice, because at first I think I'm imagining it. He's supposed to be at my sisters' tournament in New Jersey. But after two looks I'm sure it's him, sitting at the top of the stands directly across from our bench. When he sees me looking, he shouts down to me, "Way to go, Skye!" He gives me a thumbs-up sign.

The buzzer sounds. The final score is Ithaca Comets 3, Halton Hills Twisters 2. And this game has just moved into first place as my all-time favorite.

Whoa

Everyone piles out of the locker room after the game. We all wait in the lobby, clutching our first-place trophies, until Keri Nash walks in. She looks like a gymnast, not a hockey player, and she's wearing a red, white, and blue U.S. Olympic sweat suit. She has short blond hair. We follow her into this big empty room that has red carpet and a big American flag encased in glass hanging on the wall. I sit down next to Jamie and Logan on a big red, white, and blue couch.

"Hey, girls. I understand congratulations are in order!" she says.

"Yeah!" we answer, cheering.

"Which one of you is Skye O'Shea?" she asks.

My posture straightens and my face turns red. Everyone points to me. "Well, girl, step right up here and lead the way." She motions to me as she starts walking down a long red hallway. I follow closely behind, and so does the rest of my team, until we get to a door that says "USA HOCKEY: PLAYERS ONLY."

Keri punches a special code into the lock on the door and turns on the light. One by one, our team enters the room. Everyone stands silently, staring, like we can't believe where we are. The room smells like freshly cut wood. Each player has her own stall, with a gold nameplate attached above each seat. The carpet is thick, red, and clean. We walk around the room in awe. The only noise is from quiet whispers or the occasional "Cool!" or "Check this out!" Each stall is different. Some players have pictures and motivational quotes taped up, while others have stalls that are bare of decorations. All the stalls are meticulously neat and organized, with equipment carefully hung up and skates arranged neatly in a special cubbyhole. I scour the room looking for Haley's stall.

"Oh my gosh!" Sidney shouts. "Skye O'Shea, check this out!"

Everybody turns to look at me and then back at Sidney and Rachel, who are standing next to a stall in the far corner of the room. A real Olympic jersey hangs in front of them. Everyone gathers around the jersey, and I squeeze between Cleo and Anna to see.

"Awesome! That's so cool," says Cash.

And it is. I mean, it's not every day you get to see a *real* Olympic jersey. But it gets better. Keri stands up on a chair in the middle of the room and calls for our attention. "Listen up," she says. Everyone is watching her. She steps down from the chair and makes her way to the front by the jersey. She takes it off the hanger and hands it to me. "This is a special gift for you, from your friend Haley Bryce."

"Whoa!" says Logan.

"Oh. My. Gosh," says Cash.

"You're so lucky, Skye," whispers Cleo, standing right next to me. Even Abigail Dwyer smiles.

Everybody on my team is now staring at me as I slip Haley's red, white, and blue jersey over my head. "Haley wanted me to read this note to all of you," Keri says as she unfolds a yellow piece of paper.

OK, please—could this day get any better? I am in heaven. Keri passes out U.S.

Haley Bryce 17
HaleyBryce17@aol.com

Hey, Skye & team—
I hope your team is enjoying your special tour with Keri. I wish I could be there IN PERSON to show you around the Olympic Training Center. Enjoy your time in Lake Placid, have a GREAT tournament and always remember: skate hard, hustle, and have FUN! Best of luck
Go Comets!! Haley #17
"You miss 100% of the shots you don't take."
Wayne Gretzky

Olympic hockey pins, and everyone gathers around me, touching and admiring my jersey.

"BRYCE" is sewn just below the shoulders in big blue letters.

Brag Away

Draped in my new Olympic jersey, with the sleeves rolled up so that it fits me, I flop onto the front seat of my dad's truck and start talking a mile a minute. "Dad, can I tell you about my goal, even though you were there and you saw it?" I ask, smiling ear to ear. "And I want to tell you every detail!" I am barely able to stop for a breath.

"Sweetheart, that's what dads are for!" he says.

"Dad, I am so happy you were there—"

"I am, too, champ," he says, ruffling my ponytail with one hand and keeping his other hand on the steering wheel.

"Could this day have been any better?" I ask. "I mean, first I score the greatest goal of my life, then we win the tournament, and then I get the jersey in the locker room. And I'm not bragging or anything, but—"

"Hey, pal. If you can't brag to your dad, who can you brag to?" he asks.

By the time we reach the sign that reads *Lake Placid Appreciates Your Visit*, I have gone over every single aspect of my goal in minute detail. "That was the best shot I ever took!" I say.

"All those shots you've been taking before practice have paid off, huh?" my dad asks.

"Well, yeah," I agree. "I guess they did!"

"That was some goal to remember," he adds.

"Yeah. I still can't even believe it," I say, slumping back into the seat, the day catching up to me. I replay my goal a hundred times in my head and feel my eyelids beginning to close. "It was so awesome, Dad," I mumble, almost asleep.

"Well, I'm proud of you, sweetheart. And not just because you had a good game, but more because you are a class act. And your mom and I both are very proud of your attitude." Then he turns to me real quickly and winks. "You're all right, kid."

And I sleep the whole way back.

The Dance

Paige has invited Grace, Emily, and me over to get ready for another Lakeview dance. When my mom drops me off, she leans over and gives me a hug. "Have fun, honey," she says as she gives me a kiss on my forehead. "And cut a rug!" she shouts out the window as she drives away. I love my mom, but sometimes she is so weird.

Paige has one of those cool teenager rooms like you see on TV. The walls are painted light orange and the carpet is thick, shaggy, and green like grass. Besides that, she has her own stereo *and* TV right there in her room. She is so lucky. It's teenager paradise, and she's not even a teenager yet. Paige has a ton of clothes, and her closet is almost as big as my entire room.

Grace, Emily, and I all decide we will go to our very first dance outfitted by Paige. We take turns trying everything on and parading around the room like we're in a fashion show. I finally pick out a pink tank top and black stretch bell-bottom pants. Paige decides we should all wear pink sparkly glitter. She smears it on our cheeks and around our eyes. By the time we finally pack into her mom's car, even I have to admit I'm looking pretty good.

When we first walk down the long, dark hallway to the dance, it's weird. I mean, I'm not used to my school being dark and having dance music playing. I'm not used to seeing all these glittery mirror balls and pink lights in what is otherwise our boring cafeteria. Tonight, though, it has been transformed into a dance floor, and it looks really cool. In honor of Valentine's Day, there are a zillion little cutout red hearts dangling on strings from the ceiling. Paige, Emily, Grace, and I meet Olivia, Lindsay, Caitlyn, and Winnie over in the corner by the soda machines. The music is loud. A handful of kids are already dancing, but most of them are seventh and eighth graders.

I stand against the wall and scope it out. The first person I see is Isabel. She broke up with Sam last week, and she's dancing with Kevin Flynn. Isabel waves and motions me out to the dance floor, but I'm not feeling especially brave yet. Then the music slows and all these couples crowd the floor. Everyone who's not dancing with someone stops and leans against the wall like I do. So I'm standing there just checking things out when it happens.

Ashton.

He comes up to me out of nowhere. I'm not expecting it. He is looking particularly handsome. His hair is combed and trimmed, and he's wearing a blue Hawaiian surfer shirt. And even though the little voice inside my head is saying *Don't start liking him again, Skye, he has a girlfriend,* I do. I like him—a lot. All the feelings I had—and still have—are swirling in my head, stomach, and heart. I am practically dizzy by the time he speaks.

"Hey," he says. He is standing really close to me.

"Hey," I say.

"What's going on?" he asks, smiling.

"Not much," I say, trying to seem really cool and under control even though I am so not.

"Do you want to dance?" he asks.

Yeah, that's right. You don't have to read that again. This is what he asks me, right there at the Valentine's Day dance. I am surprised, too. OK, I am more than surprised—I am totally blown away, and my heart starts to pound as he grabs my hand and leads me out onto the dance floor. I look over at my friends to see if I am imagining this, but I don't see anyone.

"So, I never see you anymore," he says, both his hands resting on my hips. I place my hands lightly on his shoulders, even though this is my first slow dance and I have absolutely *no idea* what I am doing.

"Ahhh, yeah," I say, attempting to speak and dance at the same time and learning very quickly that this is hard to do. "Ahhh, well, yeah. I only go to my tutor every other week, and you have wrestling now, so I guess we can't walk together anymore, huh?" I say this all in one mixed-up breath. My conversational skills seem to have gone out the window. I glance around to see if any of my friends are witnessing this miracle of a moment. I lock eyes with Isabel, two couples away. Her head is resting on Kevin Flynn's shoulder. She is smiling and giving me the thumbs-up sign. She is clearly as shocked as I am by this recent turn of events.

"Skye?" Ashton asks. Oh, no. I think Ashton has been trying to talk to me while I am spacing out. I turn my head back and look at him. I get a big-time close-up of his tie-dye blue eyes. My heart is thumping so loud, he might actually be able to feel it if I get much closer to him.

I smile. I cannot seem to speak. This is too weird, too fun, too crazy. My hands are sweating. I move them to a new spot on his shoulders. I am not sure if I am doing this "right."

"Hey, I want to ask you something," he says, moving closer to me, now four inches away.

"Sure," I say.

"Well, I was wondering if you like anybody

right now?" he asks. He asks this real softly and quietly and gently. He is practically whispering in my ear. *I am not making this up.* It is happening just like this, and I am practically going to faint. I am looking at the guy I totally like, the guy I have been thinking about all year, the guy who I pray will like me back, and he is asking me—me—if I like anybody! I scan my brain for anything intelligent or even semi-intelligent to say.

"Ahhh" is all that comes out of my mouth. I try again. "Ahhh, well, sort of," I say, hoping that this half-truth won't be so obvious.

"Well, I know somebody who likes you," he says, smiling, "a lot."

OK, wait. This is sounding familiar. This is the same exact thing—

Oh, no.

It's Nate.

It's Nate!

I feel so stupid that I am figuring this out now on the middle of the Lakeview dance floor—which is really the Lakeview cafeteria—and I am just putting it all together. Of course! The notes, the ear-whispering thing, seeing Ashton at my locker—he was doing it all for *Nate.* It is all making sense, and right at this very moment, every single ounce of hope, joy, and light seeps out of my head, through my heart, and into my feet. I am *not* hearing the music.

"Skye? Earth to Skye?" Ashton asks, joking.

I snap out of it.

"It's Nate," he says, as if I had no idea about this matter. He is still smiling. This is apparently fun for him. "He wants you to go out with him," he says, matter-of-factly. And then the big question, the question I am absolutely dreading, comes. "Will you go out with him?" he asks. "'Cause he really, really likes you, Skye, and he wants to know."

The slow song has conveniently come to a stop just as the bomb has dropped on my little party. We are still standing, though, perfectly still, in the exact same spot where we were slow dancing. The beat is faster now. The lights are blinking. The music is loud. The room is vibrating. People are swirling around us.

"Well," I stammer for something, anything, to say that will sound nice but definite. Something that won't hurt Nate's feelings. "Well, I was kind of hoping we could just be friends, if that's all right?" I say, kind of like it's a question. "I mean, Nate's nice and everything, but I think of him more as a friend." I say this. I don't know where it comes from, but I just blurt it out and I am so thankful.

"OK, that's cool," Ashton says, still smiling. And, if you must know, he is now holding my hand, not strong and firm, but really lightly. Our fingertips are just sort of tickling together.

And then I hear it. It is a girl voice. "Excuse me," it is saying. "Excuse me, but Ashton, can we dance now or what?" she asks, impatiently.

It's Brooke Benton, and she's big-time ruining my little moment. But I don't care because Ashton and I danced. My heart is feeling light, and I'm starting to feel normal again for the first time since that hallway fiasco when I saw Ashton and Brooke kissing.

Ashton smiles at me as he lets go of my fingers and disappears into the crowd on the dance floor with Brooke. And he is *so* not my boyfriend, and he is *so* obviously with Brooke, but I don't even care anymore. Because tonight he was four inches from my face and it felt like nothing I have ever felt before. And even though he is with Brooke, I sort of get the feeling that I wasn't wrong, that Ashton really does kind of like me—that I didn't imagine the whole thing.

And I am feeling pretty good until I see Nate, who obviously hasn't checked in with Ashton yet. He walks up to me with a big smile on his face.

"Hey, wanna dance?" he asks.

"Ummm," I say, searching my brain to think of a nice way to say no. "Well, can I take a rain check?" I blurt out.

A rain check? No, I do not know where these words come from, either. But they slide off my tongue and out of my mouth, and I can't take them back. I think it's something my mom says (as in, "Skye, I can't take you to the mall today because I have to work, but how about a rain check?"). Nate looks at me. He is cute in a too-short-for-me, not-my-type kind of way.

"OK, sure," he says, shrugging his shoulders. "Some other time."

I am pretty sure he gets the message. And I am feeling bad, but not entirely bad. I think I'd feel worse if I had said yes even when I wanted to say no. I am proud of myself. I am happy.

Buffalo Bisons

Hockey is over. I managed to score one goal in our first game against the Buffalo Bisons, but otherwise we didn't do too well in the state tournament. I did not eat any buffalo wings! I will let you read about it yourself because, actually, I have to go soon. Summer's picking me up—Apple and I have lacrosse practice at Cass Park. I have good news, though, and my mom always says good news should be shared. So here it goes.

Well, number one is this—I got a B in math! Kiesha was so happy for me that instead of going over math yesterday, we walked to Purity and each got a double cookies-and-cream sundae with hot fudge and sprinkles.

And that's not all. I won the Time Capsule Project! I won $300! And it was awesome because I had completely forgotten I had even entered. Ms. Hahn called my mom and my mom was really happy. "Skye, when you put your mind to it, you can do anything!" she said.

And even though I wouldn't say my sisters are actually being nice to me, we haven't had a big blow-up kind of fight since the pro-wrestling headlock/biting incident. I think it's probably due to the fact that they aren't as stressed anymore, because they finally decided which college they are going to. I'll let you read about it in the article (which I am in, by the way, if you read it all the way to the very end). And it was cool because even though my hockey season is over, it was kind of not over because lots of teachers at Lakeview read the article and said something to me. And I already feel like next season is going to be even better.

15U Comets End Season

(Buffalo, NY) The Ithaca Comets came up empty in their run for the New York State Championship in Buffalo Saturday, dropping two games to the Buffalo Bisons and the Syracuse Stars. In the first game, the Comets held tight to the hosts and eventual tournament winners Buffalo, but couldn't hold on, dropping 4-3 in OT. In the second game, Syracuse blanked Ithaca 2-0. The Comets were outshot 42-17. In a consolation contest, the Comets beat the Niagara Coyotes, 2-1.

NHL.

The Ithaca Tribune

Ithaca's O'Shea Sisters Head for Harvard

Double Trouble for the Rest of the Ivy League
By Jay Greenberg—Tribune Staff

Ithacans Shannon and Shelby O'Shea, two of the nation's most sought-after female prep ice hockey players, signed letters of intent today to attend Harvard University in Cambridge, Mass. The O'Shea sisters announced their decision at a press conference in the Ithaca High School activities building Friday morning. "We're just really excited to be getting to play together, and to play together at Harvard, it's a dream come true," said 17-year-old Shannon O'Shea. Identical twins who have been playing hockey together since age six, the O'Sheas were known nationally as a package deal.

"We decided a long time ago that we would try to work really hard in school and hockey so that we would get the opportunity to play together in college," said Shannon O'Shea.

Both Shannon and Shelby are members of the National Honor Society and have both been honored as USA Today High School Academic All Americans. The O'Shea sisters have identical 3.9 grade point averages. "They are outstanding student athletes," said Ithaca High School Principal Michelle Hang. "They are a pleasure to be around and are truly shining stars for the Ithaca community."

The O'Sheas are daughters of local physician Dr. Gabrielle

Goldstein-O'Shea and Lance O'Shea, a Cornell professor. "We are really proud of both of them," said Lance O'Shea, a former girls hockey standout for the Big Red (Class of 1971). "I was hoping they would go to Cornell, so we'd get to see them more often, but I am thrilled with their choice and will look forward to making the trip to Massachusetts," said Goldstein-O'Shea.

Asked if they would miss Ithaca, both girls discussed their love for Tompkins County. "This will always be home for me," said Shannon. "And, don't forget," added Shelby, "there's one more O'Shea left, and she's already better than both of us were at her age!" Little sister Skye O'Shea, 11, is a sixth-grade student at Lakeview Middle School. The O'Shea sisters will showcase

Shannon O'Shea   **Shelby O'Shea**

"We're just really excited to play together, and to play together at Harvard, it's a dream come true."
~ 17-year-old Shannon O'Shea

"There's one more O'Shea left, and she's already better than both of us were at her age!"
~ 17-year-old Shelby O'Shea

their talents this summer in Colorado Springs, Col., as members of USA Hockey's Select 17 team.

Three Days Later

I am sitting in homeroom doodling on my language arts folder—daydreaming about spring, lacrosse, and hockey camp this summer—when Ms. Hahn says something that catches my attention.

"In a few minutes, someone is going to be joining us," she says. "Listen, I know it's May and it's late, and you guys all know each other already. It might be hard to have someone new join us this late in the school year, but I really hope we can make our new student feel comfortable."

Everybody is looking around.

New kids are exciting.

They don't happen too often.

"And I know I can count on each of you to do your best to welcome him," Ms. Hahn continues. My ears perk up at "him." A new boy. This is getting good.

It is at this very moment that Dr. Delaney from the guidance office appears at the door. She is not alone. A lean, athletic-looking boy with black hair and deep olive skin is standing quietly beside her. His gray T-shirt says "Wisconsin Lacrosse" across the chest. He is cute. And even though I don't know him and have never spoken with him in my entire life, there is something I like about him.

"Class, I'd like you to meet Dustin Walsh," Dr. Delaney says. Then she turns to Dustin, like he's in first grade or something. "Dustin, I'd like you to meet your new homeroom." It's awkward. Ms. Hahn jumps in. "Come in, Dustin. Why don't you have a seat anywhere you want? Just pull a desk up to our circle."

And that's when it happens. Dustin Walsh, who can sit anywhere in the entire place, who is majorly hot, pulls a chair right up to my desk. And right at this very moment, I get that heart thing, the stomach thing, and the butterfly thing all at the same time. Only, for the first time in my sixth-grade existence, this is not caused by Ashton. It's the new kid.

Ms. Hahn is talking. "Why don't we all introduce ourselves?" she says.

"Hey, I'm Tyler."

"Hi. Max."

All the students go around the room saying their names. My heart starts pounding. *Don't say anything idiotic*, my internal voice of doubt booms in my head. *Just smile. Just be normal.* The voice is particularly talkative today.

And before I know it, I'm speaking. "Hey," I say, turning to face him, flashing my most captivating smile. "I'm Skye," I say in my best

"I'm cool" voice, which I'm still working on, by the way.

"Hey," he says back, smiling for the first time. He has nice teeth. I notice this right away.

My hands are sweating. My ears are tingling.

I'm starting to like this feeling.

I think I'm going to be OK.

If you enjoyed Yours Truly, Skye O'Shea, take a sneak peek at Skye's next adventure: Skye's the Limit!

Let's Start with This

I am sitting on the bus, three rows back, sandwiched between Paige (my best friend) and Isabel (my neighbor). It's spring. It's sunny. It's the last day of school. We have no problem acting extremely silly. To top things off, I have just announced my top-secret summer plans.

"O.K., wait. Let me get this straight," says Paige. She is looking at me like I'm crazy. "You're gonna fly in a plane, all by yourself, 3,000 miles away, to go to some adventure camp where you don't know *anybody?*" She pauses dramatically. "Aren't you, like, scared?"

"Well—" I start, but Isabel jumps in.

"You're *so* lucky, Skye," she says. "I have to babysit all summer!" Isabel shuts her eyes like she's dreaming. "Three whole weeks, riding bikes around an island in the Pacific Ocean. Toasting marshmallows every night over a campfire." She turns to me and smiles. "That is just so cool. *So. Cool.*"

Paige grins. "Are there going to be any *boys* on this island?"

We all crack up. Paige is a little boy crazy. I reach down, unzip my backpack, and fish out the official Cat Island Adventure Camp catalog so they can see for themselves. Paige flips through the photos of smiling campers. "Wow! This looks fun!" she says. And it does.

When the bus comes to a complete stop at Kyle Kimber's brick driveway, Paige is still glued to the catalog. "Oh, my gosh! It says you get to swim in the ocean," she reads out loud, "and sleep under the stars!"

I stand up, sling my backpack over my shoulders, grab my language arts posters, my stuffed science notebook, and my balled-up gym clothes. Paige rolls up the catalog and sticks it under my arm. She is smiling at me.

"I just have one question for you," she says. I wait.

I struggle to not drop all my stuff. "O.K., if you're on an island in the middle of nowhere . . ." She pauses. "What do you do when you gotta *go?*" Isabel and I laugh all the way down the aisle and out of the bus. Paige yells out the bus window, "OK, I'm now officially jealous, Skye! Bye!" She waves.

"Bye, Paige!" we yell back. Isabel and I walk up the middle of the road to the row of mailboxes where our driveways meet. "So when do you leave?" she asks.

"In ten days," I say.

"Ten days! That's so soon!" says Isabel. "No hockey camp?"

"Yeah, well, my mom says I can only do one or the other, and this just sounds so . . ." I strain my brain for the right word. "So—"

"Glamorous!" says Isabel.

"Exactly!" I say. *Glamorous.*

Isabel flashes me her megabuck smile. "You're gonna have a blast," she says. She turns away and starts walking up her driveway. "And I'll write, I promise!"

The minute I walk in the door, I sprint up to my room, dump my backpack on the floor, and call my mom at work. I am already picturing myself getting on the plane, and as soon as I hear her voice, I start talking. "Mom, I decided."

"Decided? Decided what, Skye?" she asks.

"Camp!" I tell her. "I'm going to Cat Island."

"Sweetheart, that's marvelous!" she says. "It's going to be such an adventure."

"I've got to send in the application, like, soon!" I say. I am panicked. *The application is due tomorrow, and now that I've told everyone, I mean—*

"Skye, calm down," says my mom. "Listen, I already checked with the Cat Island people, and we'll just mail the application with the check tomorrow. They said that's fine."

"Are you sure?" I ask.

"I'm sure."

"Really?"

"Really."

"Thanks, Mom," I say.

"Now, go clean your room. I saw it before I left for work, and it's a pigpen!"

After I hang up, I collapse on my bed. For a split second I wonder if I should change my mind. I've gone to the same hockey camp for the last five years. It's three miles from my house. It's a sure thing, a guaranteed good time. Plus, I know everybody there, and everybody knows me. This adventure camp thing—this is kind of crazy. It's like nothing I've ever done before.

My stomach flutters, like it knows this is a momentous decision. I hang off the side of my bed and grab the Cat Island catalog. "Have the summer of your life!" it says in bold writing. *The summer of my life,* I think, smiling, and I close my eyes. *The summer of my life.*

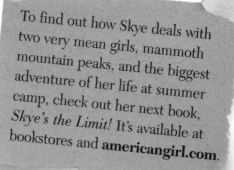

To find out how Skye deals with two very mean girls, mammoth mountain peaks, and the biggest adventure of her life at summer camp, check out her next book, *Skye's the Limit!* It's available at bookstores and **americangirl.com**.